Practical Pia wishes for her own pixie man to have and to hold on to, but she doesn't expect to wake up with him a couple of hours later. Peter has been dumped by his human girlfriend and is only too glad to salve his bruised and shaken feelings with a miss who welcomes his pixie grip.

It's lucky that Pia is up for a challenge, because Peter is a challenge and a half.

Peter is determined to marry Pia immediately. The vicar, who happens to be his grandfather, has other ideas.

While Peter and Pia begin their long and fruitful marriage, Peter's ex-girlfriend, Barbie, faces a life-altering situation.

Meanwhile, Peter's younger cousins, Salix Peter Grene and Joe Bakewell, pursue their own hopes, and Judit Creed, artist's model and dancer, entertains her favourite soldier in the dressing room.

This book is a work of fiction. Names, characters, places, and incidents either are products of the author's imagination or are used fictitiously. Any resemblance to actual events or locales or persons, living or dead, is entirely coincidental.

Peter and Pia
Copyright © 2020 Lark Westerly
ISBN: 978-1-4874-2696-5
Cover art by Martine Jardin

Published by eXtasy Books Inc or
Devine Destinies, an imprint of eXtasy Books Inc

Look for us online at:
www.eXtasybooks.com or www.devinedestinies.com

Peter and Pia
The Pixie Grip Book 1

By

Lark Westerly

AUTHOR NOTES

The *Fairy in the Bed* series has a large cast of characters who wander in and out of one another's stories. Some of them are major continuing characters, and some appear just now and then.

For a full list of who is who, who is related to whom, and a timeline for the series, check out Lark Westerly's home page at https://larksinger.weebly.com

The Peckerdale and Grene families first appeared in *Green Balls,* which was set in 2016 and which introduced the Peckerdale-Grene community tower. Their story begins long before that, though, when the young pixie man Peter Peckerdale, fresh from a failed romance with a human girl, blunders into a pixie miss named Pia. This is Peter's story, and also introduces two of his cousins, Salix Peter Grene and Joe Bakewell.

This tale, *Peter and Pia,* begins in 1950, and ends in 1956. It's the first book in *The Pixie Grip* series. *Peter G and Gentian* comes next. That one tells what happened to Peter G and his mysterious friend, Gentie. Other titles in the series continue the story of the irrepressible pixies of the tower right up until the 2020s, when the still-vigorous Peter Peckerdale is ageing disgracefully and still enjoying the time of his life, still romancing his darling Pia, and busily bothering his descendants.

A companion series, *The Red Cat,* tells the story of the priest Rory Inkersoll and his beloved Emer, beginning in 1944.

The suburb of Windhill in Sydney doesn't exist. If it did, it would be somewhere near North Sydney.

The songs *Barbara Allen, Annie Laurie* and *Me Lovien Woldë* are real. *Merrily We* is made up.

Chapter One: Barbie and the Elf

Windhill, Sydney. 1940s
Barbara Hanover

Barbara Hanover had known about elves for as long as she could remember. Sylvie Cowrie and her cousin Meredith Oak were in her class at school, and Jacobi le Fay often kicked a football around the oval with her brother Johnny.

They were elves, or maybe half-elves and she accepted them just as she accepted Julia Conti whose dad was Italian and Josh Levy whose Uncle Moshe had funny dangly bits of hair.

When they got to twelve or so, everyone started changing. The girls got taller than the boys, and annoying things happened to bodies that used to be reliable. A few painful spots popped out on Barbie's chin.

The elves changed, too, but not in the same way. They never got spots or lumpy bits, but Meredith Oak got into trouble for throwing a spoon to her cousin, and Sylvie was given detention for eating cake when she should have been writing an essay. There was a lot of enquiry about where she'd got the cake, because it wasn't from the school lunch menu. Sylvie wouldn't say.

When Barbie was fifteen, Jacobi le Fay gave her a rose and asked if she wanted to go to the pictures with him. Barbie wondered where he'd got the rose, since he hadn't had it when he came back from kicking a ball with Johnny. It was the first time anyone had given her flowers, although she wasn't sure if one single flower counted. She put it in a vase in her bedroom.

Mum and Dad talked about it and said she could go to the pictures, but only if Johnny went, too. The boys talked about football, but they agreed to her request for a comedy rather than a western, and Jacobi got her ice cream at the interval.

One day, when Johnny was having a bath after a muddy accident at the oval, Jacobi waited for him in the living room with Barbie. He was neat and clean as always.

He never seems to fall over and slide about in the mud, and he smells nice, like lemonade.

Barbie told him she wanted to go to art school. She thought it would be nice if she and the other girls could draw him at art club because he didn't have any spots or bumpy bits. He looked . . . nice. She said so, awkwardly.

"I hope it's not a life drawing class," Jacobi said.

"What?"

"I mean . . . Could I keep my clothes on?" He blushed.

So did Barbie. "You are *awful*, Jacobi."

"You're not. You're . . . I mean, I like you."

"I like you, too," Barbie said. It was all right to say it if the boy said it first.

Jacobi, still a bit pink in the cheeks, told her he had something secret to show her. It was called *disclosure.*

Barbie was wary about having a boy show her something secret, but it turned out he just wanted to demonstrate exactly how Sylvie and Meredith had thrown things and got cake at school when they were younger.

It was called conjuring, and it was something to do with being an elf. She didn't tell him she'd already known he was an elf.

Jacobi often showed her secret things after that. When they left school, he started calling to take her to the cinema more often, even without Johnny, and sometimes he kissed her in the dark. It was so nice, but Barbie was still set on going to art school. She sent away for booklets and talked to the careers adviser she'd had at school.

The best one was at a place called Appledore in Victoria, but her parents refused to let her go.

Barbie went to work for a man her dad knew, sitting in a typing room with three other girls. She saved her money and went on drawing as much as she could.

When she was nineteen, Johnny got a place at Appledore University to do medical studies. They let *him* go, and eventually, they said she could go, too, if Johnny kept an eye on her.

Jacobi was teaching her how to drive his car. He offered to drive her to Appledore, but of course, her parents said no, she had to take the train to Melbourne and then catch a bus. Then Johnny, who'd been home for the holidays, agreed to go back with them, and it was all right again.

Jacobi kissed her goodbye while Johnny fidgeted because he wanted to go and sort out his classes.

"Have fun, Barbara Allen, but not too much," Jacobi whispered.

He sometimes called her that.

She hugged him, inhaling his sweet, familiar smell. "I'll see you during the holidays."

"I'll come and visit you as often as I can."

CHAPTER TWO: PETER

Lady Lydia Appledore House, Appledore. Winter, 1950
Barbara Hanover

A rt School was fun.

Barbie, flushed with satisfaction at having finally broken free of the placid certainties of Windhill, moved in at *Lady Lydia Appledore House*, a respectable boarding hostel where students and young workers lived. Her brother lived with a classmate on the floor above for the first year. Then, as his medical studies progressed, he and his friend moved closer to the university and the hospital where he was doing his practical training.

"You'll be all right, Barbie?"

"Of course I will. I'm not a kiddy." She was nearly twenty-one. Her parents and Jacobi had wanted her to go home after her course ended, but Barbie had started a new one, which was more exciting. She worked part-time as a model for one of the teachers, wearing a playsuit so the students could see her limbs. She'd also been asked to pose for a life drawing class, but of course, she'd said no.

She almost wrote to Jacobi and told him about it, but in the end, she didn't. He'd be upset.

He came on one of his occasional visits soon after that, and they drove to Melbourne and went dancing.

Then Jacobi had to spoil it by asking when she was coming home.

"This is home, for now," she said. She indicated *Lady Lydia*

Appledore House, which was inevitably known as *LadyLyddy* by its occupants. "Would you like to come in for coffee?"

"What exactly do you mean by coffee?"

"Coffee. In the common-room. What did you think I meant?"

Jacobi thanked her and declined. He said he'd stay in Johnny's room for the night and drive home in the morning. He got out of the car.

Barbie was confused until she realised Jacobi thought Johnny was still at *LadyLyddy.*

That was awkward.

"Are you going to tell my parents?"

Jacobi looked surprised. "I don't even see your parents from one week to the next. You should tell them, though. Or come home."

They didn't part on the best of terms.

Barbie saw the new boy arrive. He got out of a car driven by a middle-aged lady. She got out, too, and passed him a bag.

She reached up to kiss his cheek. "You'll be okay, Peter. Let us know if you need anything."

"I'll be all right. Thanks for the ride. I've got to learn how to drive these fucking things."

"Peter—"

"Sorry. Keep forgetting."

"You had two years to get the language right."

He lifted a shoulder. "Yes, but that's a while ago. Bye, anyway, Prue."

She drove off, and the boy stood looking a bit lost.

He was tall, with black hair and an arresting face. His skin was a strong shade of olive.

Italian, like Julia Conti.

Barbie wanted to paint him, but what he'd said to the lady made her doubtful about approaching him.

Maybe he doesn't speak English very well.

She approached him with caution. "Hello. I'm Barbara. Barbie. Do you need any help with your things?"

He looked her over and smiled. He had a slightly crooked mouth, and his eyes were an odd colour, almost blue, but stronger and brighter. Turquoise, maybe. "Barbie. Are you human?"

She laughed. "Yes. Aren't you?"

"No."

He was odd, all right.

"Come in, and I'll show you where to register."

"I've got a room fixed," he said.

"Do you know where?"

"Third floor, number sixteen. I got the key from Prue last week."

She was impressed. The third floor was reserved for working people. It wasn't a dorm, and some of the rooms even had their own bathrooms, or so she'd heard.

"I'll help you find it," she said.

They went up the stairs and located the room. The boy touched the door, and it swung open.

Can't have been locked . . . oh, wait . . . did he conjure that?

"Want to come in?" he asked.

"No."

She did, rather.

"I'd better not," she added.

"Oh. *No harm.*"

"Of course not, but it's not really done."

"My name's Peter Peckerdale," he said, holding out a massive hand.

She shook. His hand was warm, and he smelled of fresh grass.

An elf? Could be.

"Maybe I'll see you around, Peter."

She peeped past him into the room. It had lovely light. It was much bigger than her little place with its shared bathroom where two of the other girls left their stockings and under-things hanging in the bathroom to dry.

She put away envy and went downstairs.

Barbie blamed Jacobi for what happened after that. She knew it was unfair, but if he hadn't been so stiff and disapproving after the dance, she might have gone home at the end of the term. Also, she blamed him for being an elf and for giving her an insight into that secret world of conjuring and what she thought of as magic. The elves she knew were nice people. Even Jacobi was nice when he wasn't carrying on like a Victorian papa. He was only two years older than she was, so why did he have to be so stiff?

She thought Peter Peckerdale was an elf, too, and that made her feel safe. It was Jacobi's fault for being the way he was.

Peter was an odd mixture. She'd thought he was at least her age, but he said he was just eighteen and *had enough years*, whatever that meant. He talked like a navvy. His swearing bothered her, though he never blasphemed. In other ways, he was quaintly old-fashioned.

They had coffee in the common-room sometimes, although he didn't seem to like it much. They went to the pictures, and he held her hand. He didn't know how to drive, so she taught him in Johnny's car.

Peter and Johnny got along well. Johnny said he was an interesting specimen and speculated on whether he had green blood.

Peter said he didn't, but that he sometimes went a bit green when he got embarrassed.

Barbie saw no evidence of that. Peter didn't seem to care what other people thought of him.

Then Johnny asked for a sample of Peter's blood because

Jacobi had told him things about blood and immunity.

Peter gave it to him, but he refused to go into the hospital for *tests*. "Not fucking likely."

He was looking for work, so Barbie took him to the art school and introduced him to the teacher who'd wanted models. After that, she used to find sketches of Peter's face and hands pinned to easels and gracing portfolios. He was popular among the bohemian set, who didn't mind his language. He was graceful in an odd way, and he could stand in a pose for a long time without complaint.

She heard he did some of the special poses for the life drawing and was surprised at how oddly conflicted she felt. He had every right to earn some extra money, and he was a wonderful figure to draw, but he seemed so casual about it all.

"Aren't you embarrassed?"

"Why would I be? I have a cloth over my bits, mostly."

"*Peter!*"

"You know I've got fucking bits. So have you. Nice ones." He reached for her chest, and she smacked his hand away.

"Don't."

This was happening too often for her peace of mind.

"Don't you like me?"

"You know I do." She thought about Jacobi, who had never, ever reached for her chest.

"*No harm,*" he said. He looked dejected.

"Not for you. Girls have to be careful."

"I'd be careful. I give good warmth." He kissed her, and she felt the warmth of his arms. She relaxed against him. Then he patted her bottom, and she jumped away. "No, Peter."

"Don't you like being loved?"

That startled her. He sounded sad.

"You're a dear, and maybe someday, but not now."

CHAPTER THREE: SWANSONG

Lady Lydia Appledore House. 1950
Barbie Hanover

One day Peter came to Barbie with excitement in his odd eyes. She'd decided they really were turquoise. It wasn't an illusion.

"I've been offered a fucking exclusive, Barbie!"

She winced.

"Sorry. Good, eh?"

"What kind of exclusive?"

"Thadd Appledore. Know him?"

Who doesn't?

Thaddeus Bellover Appledore was some kind of relative to the Lady Appledore who had established the hostel and who had been the first patron of the art school. He had once been rather famous, but his disreputable habits had made him notorious. In his sixties now, he was doing what he called *ageing disgracefully* and painting whenever he was sober, which wasn't often, from all accounts. He'd been blown up in the great war and survived, and although far too old to fight, he'd done something hush-hush during the last war.

"What does he want, Peter?" Barbie asked cautiously. She'd heard that quite apart from being a drunk, Mister Appledore was *that way inclined*.

"And that kind's good for us girls," a worldly student had told her. "They say you could model for him and he'd never lay a finger on you, except to shove you into position. Never even look at you except as a piece of art. Different story for the boys. They used to stay clear of him . . . most of them."

"Wants me to model for his swansong," Peter said.

"His—"

"Swansong. It's going to be a great big painting of Leda and the Swan. Hey—you could be Leda!"

Barbie was half tempted, picturing herself wearing a feather boa and a glamorous feathered gown, but when she looked up the subject in the *Encyclopaedia of Classic Art,* which one of the students lent her in a brown paper cover, she changed her mind and did her best to change Peter's. The story was shocking.

"It'll be fine," he said.

"Do you know what it's about?"

"Thadd explained."

Oh, did he!

Peter continued, "He's doing the swan as a manifesta-tion . . . only I'll be man-self in it. Told him pixie men don't manifest that way. More likely with a pisky or scatterblood, but he says I have the look he wants."

Pixie?

"I don't understand. I thought you were an elf."

He looked astonished. "No, I'm a pixie man. See? My ears are round."

A pixie? Well . . . why not? Since there are elves . . ."I know some elves back home, and they don't look like you. I just thought you might be one," she said. She told him about Ja-cobi, whom he'd not met.

"Got pointy ears, has he?"

"Well . . ."

"Could be using a glamour to hide 'em, or maybe he's got watered down blood."

She got more information from Peter. He was happy to talk. He assured her he didn't have to *lie down with* the model who would be Leda. "Just have to loom, see. Thadd wants me

10

to be a black swan, but man-form."

"Feathers?"

"No, just my hide. Are you sure you don't want to be Leda? Good pay. It'd be fun to work together. You *know* we look good as a pair. There's that photograph the maid at the movement class took of us together."

That was true. They were both tall. He was dark, and she was fair, and they made a good visual contrast. Nevertheless, Barbie shook her head emphatically.

"No, Peter. And you shouldn't do this, either. It's not respectable."

"I signed a contract. I won't model for anyone else until Thadd gets tired of painting or goes to glory."

That was another of the odd things Peter said. Barbie's granny used to say it, but she was old.

"Oh, Peter."

"I expect Judit will do it. She's under a retainer to be available to him, so he won't have to contract her especially."

Judit Creed was one of the professional models, a slight blonde with a boyish figure, cropped hair and an accent Barbie couldn't place.

"Thadd says she can do the vulnerable thing. She gets to wear a shift, only diaphanous to create illusions."

Barbie liked the sound of this less every second. Judit didn't fraternise with the part-time models. She was also a dancer at a place called *The Cats' Pyjamas,* where Barbie had never gone. Johnny had, once. He said it was fun, but he told her she'd better stay away from the place. "Bit bawdy," he'd added when pressed.

Peter went away for a few days soon after that. Then he returned and almost immediately went to his first session with Thaddeus. It was a Saturday night, and Barbie was a bit annoyed. She'd thought they might go to the pictures with

Johnny and Felicia, a nurse Johnny was seeing.

The next day Peter told Barbie about his evening.

"Just sketches so far. Then he gave us coffee. He's decided to do it as a triptych, with three poses, since Judit can dance."

"Can you?"

He looked at her oddly. "You know I can."

"I mean, arty dancing."

"How's this?" Peter slid into the splits and laid his torso along one leg, raising his left arm in a curve.

"That's going to be a shadowy wing, see," he said, talking without apparent difficulty from the odd position.

Barbie had taken ballet lessons for a little while, and she knew she could never have done what Peter did.

Peter unfolded as easily as he'd assumed the pose.

"What does Judit do when you do that?"

"She sort of curls like this." He dropped again, extending one leg and tucking his bent head into his arms. "Only she looks better because her backbone has nicer knobs on it."

"How long is this going to take?"

"About three weeks, which is fucking fast. Thadd reckons he can't go without a drink longer than that, and Judit says she won't be able to do it much longer."

"How's he paying you?"

"I have a bank account," Peter said vaguely. He added, "Grandad Alexis told me who to see last time I went home. Cranky old git, but he knows folk, and there's a pisky halfling who does stocks and things for some of us." He smiled at her hopefully. "Can we have another driving lesson? I saw the copper, and he said I could get my licence soon."

Barbie heard no more of the modelling job. Peter must have noticed she didn't like the idea, and he stopped talking about it.

As soon as he had his licence, he went off for a few days. He said he was going home to check the goats.

He didn't have a car, so he hired one, or sometimes borrowed Thadd's.

Barbie supposed this meant he was still working for Thadd, or maybe just running his errands. She didn't like to ask, but once, when they'd been to a dance and she'd had too many sherries, she said, "Does Mister Appledore ever . . . well . . . bother you *that way?*"

Peter stared at her. "No."

"Good."

Peter hadn't finished. "He wanted to lie down with me for a friendly fuck, but I told him I'm not a fucking gaylord."

"*Peter!*"

He shrugged. "You asked. I told him I could give him warmth, but nothing else. Poor old geezer said he'd take whatever he could get."

"What did you do?"

He said, "I gave him warmth. He had the horrors. I mean, the DTs. Couldn't just leave him alone."

"What?"

"Delirium tremors is what Johnny calls 'em. Too much fucking gin. That's why I stopped you at the third sherry. Don't want you getting the horrors. Fucking horrible."

Peter never drank alcohol, as far as Barbie knew. After all, he was only eighteen.

"I'll call round and see if he needs anything tomorrow."

Barbie didn't see him for another few days after that. She assumed he'd gone home again.

One day when she came home from a class, she saw Thaddeus Appledore's car parked skewwhiff by the kerb. One of the doors was open, and the key was still in the ignition. Tutting to herself, Barbie removed the key, shoved the gear stick and clicked the brake. She debated proper parking but left it be.

Peter's been drinking.

It seemed the only explanation.

Righteous indignation at his indulgence after chiding her about three measly sherries sent her upstairs to deliver the key and a lecture.

She tapped on the door.

"Peter?"

Silence.

"Peter, you left the key in the car."

Silence.

"Peter!"

"Here."

The door opened. The room was darkened.

"Peter?"

"In here." His voice sounded wrong, but he wasn't slurring.

Barbie stepped in and hesitated. Another door opened, revealing a room even dimmer.

After a few seconds, her eyes adjusted to the gloom, and she saw Peter lying on the bed in a huddle.

"Peter, what's wrong? Are you—" She sniffed the air, but she couldn't smell any alcohol. There was nothing but lemon furniture polish and the fresh grassy scent that was Peter's own.

"Thadd," he muttered.

Oh no. No.

She stepped back, unable to face what might have happened.

I warned him. I begged him to stay away.

Peter said, "He's gone to glory. I was with him. Held his hand. In the fucking hospital. Johnny was there."

"Oh, Peter."

He sniffed. "Poor old git. No one to love him. Held his hand."

Barbie went over to the bed. "Are you all right?"

"Yes. Could do with a fucking hug though. Bit cold."

She sat down, and he sat up, and they hugged. "I'll make

you some coffee," Barbie said.

"Tea."

She made it.

Peter opened the curtains.

Now she could see desperate unhappiness in his eyes.

"Barbie, can we have a friendly fuck?"

She stared at him.

"Lie down together? Please. *No harm.* I feel so cold."

"No." She left.

She was drinking sherry in the ladies' lounge at the hotel when the waif-like Judit came in and sat next to her. She ordered a glass of ginger ale.

"Sorry about Mister Appledore," Barbie said.

The young woman smiled. "So am I, love. He was a poof, but a nice old man. He was very good to me. Paid well, and he said he'd look after me in his will. I said I'd name my kid after him if it's a boy. I will, too. It's close to my grandad's name and less foreign."

Barbie must have looked startled.

Judit gestured thanks to the barmaid and said reflectively, "Told Tommy the rhythm method was only for dancing. We got some rubbers after Tolly was born, but Tommy says it's like showering in a raincoat. No use now. The horse has already bolted." She nudged Barbie. "Shut your mouth, love. You'll catch a fly. I'm married. Didn't you know?"

Barbie found her voice. "No. I didn't."

"Tommy's in the army, and we're saving for a house. Living with his mum was all right when we just had Tolly, but we want our own place soon. Tommy's got a job lined up for when he gets his discharge. Might be able to get that house now, thanks to old Thaddie. You going to marry Peter?"

"Well . . ."

Judit laughed. "He's a bit green *down there,* but I'm sure he gives you a good time. He's such a nice boy. Rough tongue on him, but he knows I'm married and he holds to the decencies. Never gropes me when we're holding a pose, and asks if I'm all right if I get light-headed. Not interested in Thaddie, either. Is he good in bed?"

"How would I know?" Barbie snapped.

"Thought you might. So, he's not getting it from you either. Hasn't he put the hard word on you ever?"

Barbie blushed.

"You turned him down, like a good girl. If you ever change your mind, you can have my rubbers to use. Got 'em in my bag. I was going to give 'em to the girls at the Cat, but you can have them. Peter's going to be cut up about Thadd."

She snapped open her bag and gave Barbie a brown paper package. "There. Now you can make Peter happy. Take his mind off things. I'd do it if I didn't have Tommy. By the way, blow 'em up before you use 'em. They might be a bit perished."

Barbie went back to *LadyLyddy* to make Peter happy. It was one of those times when the right thing to do felt wrong.

Chapter Four: A Nice Warm Grip

The Pixie Forest. Spring, 1950
Pia Tillien

Pia Tillien woke slowly to the sensation of someone squeezing her left breast. She frowned in the dark. The feeling was in no way unpleasant. On the contrary, she liked it a lot. It was a squeeze, but not a pinch. It hinted at delights just around the corner if that grip should flex and stroke. Just three things were missing from the experience to make it completely pleasurable. One was something soft and reciprocal for her to squeeze. The second was the identity of the person doing the squeezing. The third was the great question of whether this had to do with her belated birthday wish, made as she indulged in her *enough years* freedom to sleep under the stars in the pixie forest without needing to inform her dearly-loved parents of her intention. She had conjured them a note when she realised she was going to be late, but that was a courtesy and not an imperative. She was mistress of her present and of her future. She hoped that future contained a pixie man with a good strong grip.

Pia's frown tipped up into a smile as it occurred to her that she could solve all three lacks in the one operation.

Whoever the squeezer was, he was behind her, sharing her blanket in the pixie forest on a balmy spring night.

It was definitely a *he.* The possessive hand was large and broad palmed, big enough to handle most of her breast, so his fingers touched her ribs.

Pia, who was as flexible as any pixie miss, got her uppermost arm around behind her and groped about until she found her objective.

Ah. Nice. She slipped her fingers around it and squeezed.

Got you. Mm. Mine. Her mind slipped contentedly towards sleep, but that wouldn't do just yet. She'd made a wish, and if it was in the process of being serviced, she'd better see what the universe had sent for her delight.

She squeezed harder and purred as the hand on her breast tightened in response.

His breathing changed, and she heard a little hiss of surprise.

"You have a good warm grip there, my dear," she said.

Disconcerted silence followed her words, and the hand slackened.

"No, don't let go." She hitched forwards after the retreating hand. "Squeeze like this," she invited and demonstrated her grip as an example.

Again, she heard the intake of breath.

"Excellent grip. Can you manage just a bit harder?" she encouraged.

Tentatively, the hand closed again.

Ahhh. Contentment returned.

"Who are you?" Pia asked.

When there was no response, she rolled over to lie on her back and turned her face towards her unseen companion.

The stars were out, but this deep in the forest, not much light penetrated the trees.

The catch of breath came again, and this time she identified it as something other than surprise. "Are you crying?"

"Yes. Fuck it. Can't help it." The short response came out muffled, as if through gritted teeth.

"Why are you sad?"

"My —" He swallowed audibly.

"My?" She let go of his willy and moved her hand to his thigh to stroke the tensed muscles. "Tell me, and maybe I can make it stop."

"My miss, I mean my *girlfriend*." That word sounded savage.

Girlfriend.

Pia frowned. A girlfriend wasn't part of the plan. Either that girlfriend went out of his life, or he went out of hers, wish service or not. She kept her voice level and reasonable.

"I hope you're not human, my dear. Not that I've anything against humans, but I don't want to lie down with one, especially one with a girlfriend," she said.

"You're not lying down with a bloody human."

"Why are you talking like one then?"

"My girlfriend is human. Barbie. That is, she *was* my girlfriend. For a little bit. Now she says she's not going to be with me anymore. She doesn't like . . ." His words trailed off, and his hand tightened convulsively.

Pia curled her toes. It was lovely. She wanted him to go right on squeezing, but she'd better get a few things straight first.

"My dear, what have you done with your human? She's not rambling around *over here* unescorted, is she? That kind of thing leads to trouble with tree lads."

"Left her in Appledore," he said. The trembling in his voice had steadied, and his fingers flexed with more attention.

"So, you left her *over there* and came *over here* to get over your attack of soul-cold. Is that right?"

"Yes. It fucking well *hurt*."

She noted the past tense verb with relief. Maybe she could keep him.

"Are you going back to love Barbie at any point in your future?"

"At no bloody point. Never. There is no point. She caught the bus. Said she was going home to Sydney. S-said never to contact her again."

Phew.

"What's your name, my dear?"

"Peter."

"And have you enough years for me to be doing this for you?" She let her fingers shift back to his willy, gently stroking.

He snorted. "Plenty. I'll be nineteen in winter."

That meant he was about eighteen and a half, which was half a year older than she was.

"My Peter," she said. She liked that name. It was strong, simple and direct. It had a good meaning. She liked his voice, and his manner of speaking, which was abrupt and to the point. She liked his smell, which was like fresh grass. She *really* liked his grip on her breast. "Peter, why are you here on my blanket?"

"You said I could be here."

"I didn't say yes or no. I went to sleep on my own and woke up with you. You shouldn't just *assume*. What if I'd been a courtfolk lady?"

He sighed. "Fuck it. I should have said *you didn't say I couldn't*. I was coming through the trees, and I couldn't see much. Then I saw a kind of blur, and I stopped, and it was you, so I . . ."

She waited with interest for him to continue. When he didn't, she said, "Why didn't you conjure a lantern?"

"I did."

"Why couldn't you see me, then?"

"My — damn it to hell — my eyes are swelled up. The lantern just made it dazzle. It hurts."

Present tense. Poor man.

She recalled he'd been crying. There was still a rasp in his voice that hinted at sobs not too far away.

"So, you just decided to lie down here with me to share some warmth."

He sniffed. "I thought you were a tree maid. I'd made a wish. I laid myself down. You didn't say *greet you, sweet man,* the way the maids do, but you didn't push me away either. You pressed into my hand."

Ah!

"What did you wish, exactly?"

"I wished I wouldn't have to hurt so much ever again. Tree maids make you feel better. They don't mind if you share warmth. They *like* to help."

"That explains that," she said.

"But you're not a tree maid, so I got it wrong."

"Nothing's wrong. I'm a pixie miss. My name's Pia Tillien, daughter of Gard and his lady Tess."

"I'm a fucking pixie, too," he said glumly.

"I know that, you numpty. You have the pixie grip. It's a splendid one."

"I didn't—I don't—I didn't expect it to be like this. Having to hold something when I sleep with a maid."

"I'd guess your human maid didn't expect it either," Pia said sympathetically.

"She said it was weird. Perverted. She said it hurt. She wanted me to stop, but I—" His hand slackened again.

"You couldn't stop. I expect you tried, but when you were asleep, you just anchored on to the nearest soft part. Well, how could you not? You're a pixie man. Naturally, you have the pixie grip, and you hold on to your lover when you're asleep. It's the right thing to do. You should definitely do it." She pushed her arm against her body, making her breast flex in his hand and spoke as soothingly as she could.

"You *like* it?" he said after a few seconds.

"Mm. So nice, even though technically you're not asleep anymore." She wriggled closer. "Peter?"

"Yes?"

"Since you're here, and I'm here, and you've already pleased me, and we both wished, would you like to have a friendly with me?"

"A friendly fuck, you mean?"

"If that's the term you like to use. Mind, this is only if your human maid really doesn't want to see you again. There's no point in me making you happy if it makes someone else unhappy. If she's of a resurgent nature, the offer is off the table, and you're to get off my blanket."

"She said she doesn't ever want to see me again."

"She screamed at you? Cried at you?" Humans did that, she knew.

"No. After she got over yelling at me, she was kind about it. She sat down, and *we talked it over*. That's what *she* called it. She even kissed me goodbye."

Pia relaxed. That sounded like a totally dead love affair to her. She let go of his willy, and she said, "Let me go now."

He let her go. He didn't want to, she could tell, but he did it.

"Lie still a bit." Pia sat up and conjured off the tunic and pixie pants she'd been wearing. She twisted and put her hands on Peter's chest.

Smooth. Nice. Bare.

She ran her hands over his shoulders and touched his face. He had a strong jaw and high cheekbones. His brow was strong, too. His cheeks were sticky, and her fingers winced away from the puffiness of his eyes. He'd been telling the truth when he said they were swollen.

"I'm going to try to make your eyes feel better, so just lie still and let me tend to you," she said. She had salve at home, but she thought that would probably sting his sore skin. She remembered something that had worked when her sister, Alba, was younger and got sand in her eyes. Pia had conjured it out, but the stinging had the little maid in tears. There was just one thing for it, and Pia had done it for her sister. Now she'd do it again for her Peter.

She cupped her hands around his face. His hair felt springy

and strong. She looked forward to running her fingers through it, but she had other business first. She bent forward from her waist to kiss his damp cheek before she touched her tongue to the soft skin under his right eye. He stiffened, so obviously, it hurt. Pia licked the salt away and moved to his closed eyelid. She didn't mind the taste of tears, being quite familiar with her own and Alba's. Tears were good. They were healing, up to a point. Poor Peter's had gone way beyond that point.

When he stopped flinching, she turned her attention to the other eye.

Presently, he relaxed.

"Better, my dear?"

"Fuck me, yes!"

The catch of his breath sounded different now.

Pia bent her elbows and let herself down to lie beside him, with a hand on his chest. "Peter, why are you bare?"

She felt him squirm uneasily.

"Tell me. It's not usual unless you've been swimming."

"Water lads never wear anything. Tree lads often don't."

"You're not a water lad or a tree lad."

"If you must have it, I was dressing human to please Barbie. After she left, I came *over here* and dumped those clothes at the gateway. I *never* want to dress human again."

"You could have conjured some proper clothes."

He squirmed again. "I couldn't do it. I managed the lantern, but that was all. My focus is shot. I'd gone cold."

Past tense again. Good.

"I'll get you something of Dad's to wear. He's a fix-it pixie, so he'll be delighted to share."

"Don't bother."

"Don't be stubborn. If I'm going to keep you, I'll not have you being foolish or wandering about the forest unclothed. It would reflect poorly on me as your miss."

"Oh." He sounded uncertain.

"Oh, what?"

"Are you going to keep me?"

"I'm not sure. You said you wished never to have to hurt like that again. If I keep you, I can guarantee you will *never* hurt like that again. I will appreciate you. I want a man with a strong pixie grip, as long as it comes with a loving nature. I will do anything I can to help a man like that to be happy. I mean *anything*."

He didn't respond, so she continued. "I am a stubborn maid. I'm practical. I'm clever. I have ideas, and I make them happen. My sister says I'm bossy. I am. I like to be busy, and I like to have challenging projects. Keeping a pixie man con- tented is a project challenging enough for any miss, and I think you might be an even better challenge than other pixie men. If I keep you, I will be faithful, and I won't be difficult over petty things. I'm never petty. If it's a big thing and you're wrong and I'm right, I will be so difficult you can't even im- agine, so you might as well make up your mind to give in right away. My big things will never be unreasonable. To be sure I really am right, you can call on any other reasonable person for an opinion."

"Good to know." His voice sounded better. Then he said, "You said we *both* wished."

"So, you *were* listening to what I said. I thought you were off in misery-land."

"Of course, I was listening. You offered me a friendly, and I want to have it. I fucking need it. You can't think how much I need it. What did you wish for?"

"A pixie man of my own to have and to hold forever." She chuckled. "I didn't expect to wake up with him a couple of hours later, though."

"Can I have that friendly now?"

"*May* I," she corrected.

"May I have that friendly now? Please?"

"*We* shall have that friendly now."

He brought up one hand to trace her features. When he got to her mouth, she bit his finger.

"Ow. What was that for?"

"You were checking what I look like. Looks are immaterial. I'm not ill-favoured. I'm also not reckoned pretty. They say I'm handsome in my way, but that doesn't matter, and I'll change as I age anyhow. You can have a look at me in the morning."

"I'm not pretty either. Humans stare at me, and not . . . They recognise me, you see."

"You have far too much chin to be handsome, but I'd rather too much chin than too little. Mine is moderate, but I'm much more stubborn than that implies. Now stop wasting my time." She rolled in towards him and wrapped both arms around him, with one low enough to get a good grip on his bum.

"Ow."

"Stop squawking. I didn't hurt you." She wriggled impatiently.

He put his arms around her, too, and squeezed.

She raised one knee and used it to part his and then brought one hand around to grip his willy. It pulsed in her hand, and she gave it a good tugging.

"No *ow*?" she questioned.

He groaned. "Fuck, that's good. You'd better stop, though, or you won't get yours, and in a friendly, you *have* to get yours. I won't feel good if you don't. Barbie never —"

"Hush. I'm Pia, not Barbie. I shall most certainly get mine. You're going to be in charge of ensuring that, and I want you clear-headed enough to do it properly, and not in an unseemly rush. Therefore, you get yours first." She kneaded him and squeezed rhythmically. "How does that feel?"

"Oh, fuck, oh fuck, oh — How am I going to be able to — oh, *fuck*." He jerked against her, and she tightened her grip before she jack-knifed and clamped her mouth around him.

"You'll have to use your imagination as to *how*," she mumbled. He tasted lovely, clean and fresh.

"Oh, fuck, oh . . . oh . . . oh!"

She squeezed his bum with both hands and sucked with enthusiasm. He stopped jerking. Waves of pleasure came off him, making Pia dizzy. Suddenly, he stiffened, shuddered and shot.

When she felt him relax, she loosened her grip and sucked gently for a while. She tingled all over with anticipation.

He was panting with long gulps of air.

When his breathing slowed, Pia let him pop out of her mouth and gave his wet willy a gentle pat. "Very nice. Did you enjoy that, my dear?" She was addressing the willy, but it was the pixie attached to it who answered.

"Oh, fuck!"

She frowned in the dark. "I hope your vocabulary doesn't run only to that, Peter."

He swallowed. "No. But, oh, *fuck*, that was good. I never imagined anything could feel so good. I wanted it to go on forever — but — "

"But?" she prompted.

"But I needed to let go. So, I did, and it went on for a bit longer anyway. That was the best bit. You really enjoyed it, too?"

"I did, and I'm glad you're satisfied. Now I need to be satisfied." She waited to see what he'd do next.

He sat up, and she felt a draught of air as he opened his arms. She leaned into them and uttered a muffled squeak as he hoisted her around to sit with her back against his chest. He put one arm around her waist and moved his legs apart, carrying hers with them. Once he had her positioned, he hitched backwards, so she was sitting on the blanket between his thighs with her legs hooked over his.

He bent around her and folded down to kiss her thigh.

Pia leaned back and closed her eyes as his fingers roamed up her thighs to touch her wet centre.

He sighed with apparent pleasure and played with her for a while. Then he moved back more, so she was flat on her back. He got up and came to kneel between her knees, put a hand on each breast and bent to thrust his tongue into her. Pia let him do what he wanted, enjoying every warm stroke of his tongue.

She moaned and arched her back to encourage him. He brought one hand down to support her hips and delved in.

She opened her mouth to express approval and squealed instead as everything broke loose.

He held her hips and then lowered her gently and dropped a kiss on her belly. "Was that what you wanted?"

She swallowed, still trembling with after-shocks.

"Pia?"

"Mm. Give me a minute."

He kissed her several times and then moved up to lie beside her and lifted her into his embrace.

"Was that—"

"*Yes.* Perfect. Do I taste nice? You do."

He laughed breathlessly. "You smell like those purple and white flowers, the long ones, but you taste more like nectar."

"Those flowers are wisteria," she said, hugging him. "Now I want to go back to sleep. I do hope you'll still be here in the morning and not go slipping away in the night. I haven't nearly finished with you."

He laughed again. "Fuck that! I'm going nowhere. I want to be with you every morning, and besides, if I leave you alone, some other green-willied fucker might find you."

"And?"

"And you might give him a fucking friendly, too. And I'm *not having that.*" He turned her to spoon against him and tucked an arm right around to grasp her breast.

Pia was aware she needed to remonstrate with him, but instead, she lifted one leg and groped about for his limp willy, which she pulled forward between her legs. She got a good hold on it, conjured a second blanket from her chamber at home, and fell into sleep like a stone into a warm pool.

CHAPTER FIVE: PERSEVERANCE

The Pixie Forest. Spring 1950
Pia Tillien

When she woke from the best sleep she ever remembered, she was still holding that willy, but it was no longer limp. Pia clamped her thighs around it and stroked its silken length with pleasure.

"Are we having another friendly now?" Peter sounded hopeful.

"We are, but we might try something different."

"How different? What we had before was wonderful."

"Together, and right way up," she said.

"With me inside you?"

"Yes. I haven't done it that way yet." She kept on stroking as the willy expanded, rubbing against her pleasantly and insistently. She felt her breath coming faster and made up her mind to be straightforward. "I haven't done it at all aside from last night, so if I'm a bit clumsy this way, you'll have to be patient."

"Never at all?" He sounded disconcerted, and the willy wilted a little.

"I didn't have enough years until last week, and I wanted to get a wish match. There seemed no point in playing with anyone else. Stop that wilting. It's unbecoming." She gave him a pinch.

He caught his breath. "You'd better go on top. I'm heavy."

He moved away from her, and she felt him settle on his

29

back. "If you roll on top of me, you can either crouch or just lie on your front."

"Which is better?"

"If you lie on your front, it's easier to kiss. If you crouch, you'll have more control."

Pia considered the options. "We haven't done any kissing yet."

"We'd better fucking well start. We'll do a proper pixie smooch. It'll be bloody lovely." He sounded fierce and cheerful.

"I'll lie on you, then, and we'll see how we go." She rolled over onto her other side. It was very early morning, and the first light was just fingering its way through the leaves. They were well off the path, and Pia wondered suddenly why Peter had been walking through dense forest instead of keeping to a track. She was about to ask him when she realised she could see his face. She stopped to take stock. Looks really didn't matter, but she was interested to see if her fingers had given her a true report of his.

His was a face of strong planes and shadows, but there was just enough light for colours to emerge. She contemplated him for a good half minute. He had black hair, growing in a rough but gleaming thatch. The strong jaw and well-defined brow she'd noted were present, along with high cheekbones and a commanding nose. She thought his eyes were an odd colour, although it was difficult to be sure, since his pupils were dilated.

She held her breath and *read* him a little.

Pride, pain, hope and generosity. Impatience. So what's not *there?* She focused again and tried the more difficult reading for absence. *No deceit, no vanity and not even a hint of unkindness. Not much perception. No . . .* how odd! *There's no childishness. He just wears his feelings on his face. He's always been like that. He'll never change. Good.*

"What?" he said.

She must have been staring at him for too long.

She said, "You have turquoise eyes."

He looked nonplussed. "You want to talk about my fucking eyes?"

"Language, Peter."

"That's the way I talk."

She said, "Very well, but try to moderate it in public."

"The goats don't care. Peter G doesn't care. Thadd liked it."

Goats? Peter G? Thadd?

"I don't suppose goats would. Who is Peter G?"

"My —" He hesitated as if genuinely uncertain.

"How do you think of Peter G?"

"My best friend."

"Who's Thadd?"

"A nice old geezer who painted me and went to glory. Why do you want to discuss my eyes?"

"I have a vested interest, since I eased the swelling for you."

He smiled, showing large and excellent teeth set in a wide and slightly crooked mouth. "You did more than ease it. You fixed it. You're a capable miss. Why did you do that for a stranger?"

"You were hurting."

"That wasn't your problem. I hope you don't feel the need to soothe the hurts of every green-willied fucker you encounter."

"I wanted you to feel better. I wanted you focused on what I was doing for you and what you were doing for me, not on how much your poor eyes hurt. So, you see, it was mostly self-interest."

"Good. If I can rely on you to act with self-interest, I'll know where I am. And yes, my eyes are more or less turquoise. And no, I have no braesider in my bloodline. It's pure pixie. I just happen to have turquoise eyes. I'm the only one I know who has. Even Grandad Alexis doesn't have turquoise, though his are a fucking peculiar colour. Practically purple."

"Random mutation, then. I like it. It adds distinction," she said.

As if you needed any more of that, my Peter! No one could ever forget your face, and it will get even better as you get more years. Not handsome. Beautiful.

He took her chin in one hand and gazed into her face. "Green eyes. Brown hair. Straight nose. Good chin." He turned her face to the side. "Fine cheekbones and neat ears. I thought you said you weren't pretty?"

"I'm not."

"Will you settle for beautiful, then? Your mouth is fucking gorgeous."

She was entranced. "So, we're both beautiful. We'll have lovely children."

"You want to start one now?" He sounded interested rather than alarmed.

"Not for my first time. No. I'll tell you when. Until then, you can hold your swimmers."

"I didn't last night."

"Just as well I helped you that way, then. This time, you hold hard. Or else."

"I will." He tapped her lips with his forefinger. "Want to start with the kissing now, before you lie on me?"

"No. I'll lie on you right now, and that will save time getting organised."

He helped her to roll on top of him. "Legs apart, and don't worry. I won't shove it into you like a billygoat. We'll wait until you say."

She parted her legs and lifted her face to be kissed. She thought he'd be good at it. He was. The pixie smooch was everything she'd ever heard it was, but even better.

They kissed for a while, and Pia felt herself growing steadily more excited. Not wanting to wait longer, she wriggled down, reached around and seized his willy. Once she had it into position, she tried to squirm on to it.

"Ouch."

Wrong angle.

Peter noticed. "Fuck it! What are you doing, woman?"

She panted. "I'm sure you can guess."

"Here. Let me help." His large hands came down to clamp her thighs, and he moved up slowly. "Relax. Hold on to me as tightly as you can."

"Will that help?"

"Shit, how would I know? I just want you to hold on to me. It feels good."

She got one hand under him and grabbed his bum.

He kissed her and entered her a little way.

Pia pulled her mouth away to say, "Ow."

"Stop squawking," he said, which was fair enough as she'd said it to him. Then he said, "Fuck it, you're tight. It's like trying to stuff a carrot into a radish skin. Want to stop?"

His tone implied that he hoped not.

"Persevere," Pia said, through clenched teeth.

"Relax your bits."

"Which bits?"

He pushed harder and was suddenly in her right up to the hilt.

Pia opened her mouth to yell, but he kissed her again, holding her tightly.

She kissed him back. That helped a lot, and she felt herself liquifying and softening. He noticed that, too.

"That's right, shit, that's lovely, only I need you to open your legs more."

She did so, which apparently made more room.

"Is it hurting much, my miss?"

Not wanting to answer, she went for his mouth again and stuck her tongue inside it. He moved his hands down her sides and stroked her thighs.

She relaxed more, but something still felt odd. She pulled

her face back. "Peter?"

"Mm?"

"Can I lie on my back instead?"

He let go of her and pulled out, then rolled them onto their sides. "I'll put my hands under you. Lift your knees. Let me know if I'm too heavy. Don't want to fucking squash you."

She agreed, and they rolled again. Pia raised her knees, and he pushed in again. It was still tight, but easier this time.

"Better?"

"Ow. *Ow.* Yes, a bit."

He slipped his hands under her bum and lifted her to an angle.

"Yes! *Yes!*" she said excitedly. It was better. It was much, much better. She braced her heels and lifted higher, and the tide broke over her.

Peter lowered his face and kissed her sweetly while he speeded up until he stiffened and shuddered. She put both arms around him in the tightest hug she could manage.

They lay like that for a while, and then he rolled off and brought her up to lie in his arms. She felt him kissing her eyes and realised she must have cried a bit with pain and reaction.

She snuggled against him. It had hurt, but he'd been so kind about it. He'd offered to stop. He'd agreed to the change of position. *Not selfish, then.* He smelled wonderful.

"Pia?"

She blinked. She had the impression she'd been somewhere else for a while.

The sun had managed to pierce the branches above, and they lay in a patch of gold light. She stretched against him and pushed their covering away. He pulled it back.

"I need to get up."

He said, "I need you to stay here. Don't leave me. Please."

"I have to pee."

"Fuck it, so do I."

"Come on, then, and we'll go together."

They got up and walked a few steps away from the blankets.

Pia crouched into the proper position and, uncharacteristically, she wobbled. Her legs felt strange, and she toppled sideways.

Peter caught her and steadied her. "I'll look after the balance bit. You look after the piddling. Relax. I won't let you fall, and it doesn't matter if you splash me. I've been splashed by experts. Bloody Snick, that's the boss billygoat, likes to spread his splashes around." He crouched behind her, holding her and resting his cheek on the top of her head.

Pia felt a rush of warmth as her bladder emptied, and another rush of warmth pouring from Peter to her. She gasped as reality hit her.

He loves me. Maybe only generally, but it's a start.

"What the fuck's wrong now?" Peter asked. He unfolded his knees and helped her to her feet, and then he swung her up into his arms and carried her back to the blanket. "Can't have you standing in a lake," he said, folding again to lay her down.

"I didn't make a lake. A puddle at the most."

"I need a pee, too, remember. Trust me. It'll be a fucking lake."

He gave her a swift grin, kissed her, and moved off, not far, to do his business. He came back shaking his willy. Pia saw it was of impressive proportions, even when off-duty. No wonder it had been a tight fit.

Glad I didn't see that before I offered him the first friendly.

Having satisfied himself it was drip-free, he got under the blanket with Pia. "That was some pisserfall," he said, tugging her into his arms.

"A—"

"Pisserfall. Waterfall made of piss."

"Charming," Pia said, snuggling against him.

"What's he got to do with it? Have you been hobnobbing with hobs, my miss?"

"I have no idea what you mean. I know some hobs, certainly, but I haven't hobnobbed with them, whatever that means."

"Letting them put their knobs in . . . no, fuck it, that was your first time. A hob knob probably wouldn't fit anyway. They're big buggers. At least, I haven't looked at their knobs, but they're big all over, I should think."

"Why are we talking about hobs?"

"You started it."

"I did not."

"You mentioned Matt Charming. He's a hob. A vicar, or a bishop or something, but that doesn't stop him knobbing. Come to think of it, he's got a human wife, so she probably won't share his knob anyway. Knows Grandad Grene 'cause they're both fucking vicars."

"Is that Master Berryman Grene?" Pia asked, fixing on the last point in this incomprehensible ramble.

"That's right." He stroked her hair. "You're really sticky. Do you want to wash or something?"

"No. I want to go on doing this for a while."

"Talking about hobs?" He kissed her forehead.

"No, you numpty. *This*." She pushed her face into his neck.

He asked, "You all right, Pia? You were crying, and you nearly fell over."

"I'm all right," she said into his shoulder.

"Good. I want you to be all right. I want you to feel fucking marvellous. I want you to feel . . ."

She knew he was still talking, but another wave of warmth broke over her, and she turned mind and body to absorbing as much of it as she could.

"Pia?" He must have asked her a question because he'd

stopped stroking her and he apparently expected her to say something.

"Are we still talking about hobs?"

"Forget hobs. Please . . . I've got to know. Are you going to keep me?"

She blinked, safe and warm in the cave of his arms. "Of course, I am."

"There's no fucking *of course* about it," he said.

"Why wouldn't I want to keep you? You're lovely, and you're all mine. I'm going to feed you and kiss you and bed you and snuggle with you and probably fight with you for the rest of our lives."

"Can we start now?"

"What, snuggling or fighting?"

"I would like another friendly."

"Well, you can't have one. Or rather *you* can, but I want to have time to get over the one we just had." She paused. "Would you like me to give you another one like the one you had last night? I can do that."

"No. I'd rather wait until you feel like doing it, too. It'll be better next time. You can go underneath from the start." He kissed the side of her head. "Pia?"

"Mm?" She inhaled his warm scent, and her heart seemed to melt and overflow with happiness, which was odd, considering she was both sore and sticky.

"I want you to keep doing that."

"What?"

"That. What you're doing in there under my neck. I—" His voice broke, and he swallowed. His arms tightened, and he kissed her head again.

She pushed her face in closer and kissed under his chin. "You what?" she mumbled, inhaling so her breasts pushed against his chest.

"I want to wed you now. Quickly. Before some other green-willied fucker starts looking at you. I couldn't stand that."

Pia reluctantly came up for air. She put her hands on Peter's shoulders and pushed him away a little so she could focus on his face. He was flushed, and his eyes were dilated and strained.

Not quite in his right mind. He's afraid he'll lose me.

Nevertheless, there was something she needed to say to him. "You stop that foolishness right now. It's possible some green-willied fucker, as you put it, *will* look at me. I'll probably look a bit more tempting now I have my years."

"I'll knock him into next week—"

"You will not. You will bear with it as graciously as I will bear with it when maids and misses and lassies stare at you. I'm sure they do. It doesn't matter how many willied fuckers, green, brown, pink, black or whatever, look at me, because looking is all they ever get to do. Get that? Looking is *all* they get to do, and they're welcome to it. Whereas *you*, Master Peter, get to look and to touch and to kiss and to get your willy sucked and to enjoy a reciprocal pixie grip every night from now on."

His eyes gleamed with sudden hope. "I get to sleep with you *every* night? From *now on*?"

"Tonight and every night. Now I've had *this* I don't want to sleep without it. I don't want to sleep without you in my bed. You're my wish match and my man. Understand?"

He nodded. "So can I—"

"*Yes*, anything," she said recklessly.

He closed in and kissed her, then tucked her face into his neck. She felt him relaxing into the sensation of being wanted, just as he was. "Still want to wed you soon," he mumbled.

Might as well wed him now as later. It'll keep him from obsessing over whether I might leave him.

Pia curled in closer, reached down between them, and got a good grip on his thumb.

I wonder if he can conjure his own clothing now, or should I get him something of Dad's? I'm not taking him to meet Dad and Mum in just his skin.

She snorted in mental amusement at the thought of her mother's raised brows if she presented her pixie man dressed in nothing but a slightly crooked smile, then went to sleep.

Chapter Six: Gard's Position

The Pixie Forest. Spring, 1950
Peter Peckerdale

Peter shared a dip with Pia in one of the tiny pools that dotted the pixie forest. She resumed her tunic and pants, and he conjured his favourite pixie pants and a shirt from his old room at his parents' house. The relief of being clad once more in proper clothing should have soothed him, but as soon as he had them on, he wanted them off again, so off they came.

"Peter? Why have you taken your clothes off again?" Pia stared at him with perplexity shining from her lovely green eyes.

He reached for her, and she came to him willingly. He lifted her tunic and put his arms around her bare waist, scowling with the effort of giving words to his feelings. "I don't want anything between you and me. I can't be that far from you."

She looked up at him. "I understand, and when we go to bed tonight, there won't be anything between us. This is daytime, though."

It was the middle of the afternoon. Peter felt hollow inside but not with dismay. Without further thought, he conjured goat's cheese, radishes and some pickled onions from the larder in his mother's old cottage.

Peter G must have been there with supplies again. *Good lad.*

Pia kissed him gratefully, making his heart twinge. "How did you know I was hungry?"

"Well, I fucking well am."

"Put your clothes on before we eat."

Her voice was mild, but he perceived she meant it. He put his clothes on.

She conjured bread and cider, which he had forgotten, and they ate companionably.

"Where do you think we should go now?" Pia asked, accepting a large lump of gingerbread he'd found in his pocket. She broke it in two and handed half back to him.

Somewhere I can have you to myself forever.

He knew she wouldn't agree to that, so he pushed the thought away and said, "Have you been living with your family?"

"Yes, ever since I came back from being sponsored *over there*. You?"

"I've been living *over there* for a while. Barbie and I lived in a fucking boarding house. Lady Lydia Appledore House. I was in a bigger room up two floors, and then we sort of shared that room for a bit before she gave me the push."

Pia's face went still, and she put out a hand to him. "I'm so sorry. I didn't think."

He shrugged. "There's nothing to be sorry about. It didn't work. I should have known better than to get mixed up with a stupid bloody human. Should have waited for you."

"I have human friends *over there*. They're not stupid," Pia said.

"We're not going to need them anymore. I never want to see any of them again, and neither do you."

Pia's eyes went from sad to furious, sparking with vengeful green flame. "I am keeping my friends. You are keeping your friends. You will never, at any time, ever, have any say about what I do or who I choose to do it with as long as it doesn't affect the things that are privately ours. The same obviously applies to me in regards to your friends and activities. Is that clear?"

She meant it. One misstep now and he could lose his be-witching new miss even faster than he'd lost Barbie.

Peter fought down the surging tide of jealousy and des-pairingly faced a second dose of soul-cold in as many days. He'd been sad when Thadd went to glory, but Barbie had come to him. She'd walked out when he begged for some warmth, but she'd come back, and he'd thought she really loved him. Maybe she had, a bit. She'd lain down on the bed with him, and he'd woken when she pushed him violently away.

There had been arguments and recriminations. Barbie had stayed. He'd thought she felt she had some obligation to make it work once they'd lain down together.

He'd loved the closeness and hated the rubber things she made him wear over his willy. He'd tried to explain he wouldn't give her a baby unless she wanted one.

She'd said that was what all the boys said.

They might have weathered it all, but they couldn't weather the pixie grip. He had to hold on to her breast when he was asleep. She hated it.

He braced himself in the face of Pia's anger. He'd lost Bar-bie over the pixie grip. That was something essential to him and impossible to her. What if he lost Pia over something equally essential — his desire to possess his miss? He couldn't control one essential. Could he possibly control the other?

But I didn't need to keep Barbie to myself. She used to go out with Judit and visit Johnny. I used to go out and come over here some-times.

He couldn't understand it.

"Don't look like that," Pia said.

"What if I forget I'm not to grab?"

"That's a fair question. What do you think will happen if you forget and start trying to hoard me?"

"You'll leave me."

She waved her hand, dismissively. "Of course, I won't

leave you, my Peter. If I wanted an easy man, I'd have wished for a . . . oh, a teg, maybe. Or an elf man. They're lovely. If you forget and start grabbing, I'll remind you it's not to happen, that's all. I expect I'll want to spend a lot of time alone with you, anyway. I'm not giving up my friends and my family, but you and our children will come first with me. Your friends and family are important to you, too, and I will accept that, always."

Peter pulled himself together. He tried to come up with an answer that would make her see he could share her. "Since you've been living with your family, we might go to see them now. We can tell them what we're going to do. And then we might go to my grandfather and get him to marry us."

"And then?"

He said, "Mum has a cottage where she used to live before she wed Dad. I keep my goats there and do the garden. She said I could use it."

"You've been *over there,* though."

"Yes, but I've come back sometimes, and Peter G has been looking after it."

"What—living there? I don't want to live with your friend."

Peter chuckled, thinking of Peter G. "Pete lives with Uncle Quercus and Aunt Russet. He just said he'd see to the goats and garden. We could live there for a while."

Pia said, "Is the bed a big one?"

"Not very. Is that a problem?"

"The very opposite. I don't want to lose you in the night."

"Fuck, no!"

She took his hand, raised it to her lips and kissed his fingers. Then she said, "Come and meet Mum and Dad and Alba, and then we'll go to Master Grene."

"Who the fuck is Alba?"

"She's my younger sister. She's a gentle miss, so she will

probably find you intimidating. If you can hold off with the language, she'll like you better."

"I'll try. Are there any more of you?"

"No, just me and then Alba. What about you? Brothers? Sisters?"

"Just me."

"And your friend. Another Peter. Isn't that confusing?"

He laughed. "Fuck, no! It's a family name. I'm older, so it's my first name. Peter G's younger, so it's his second name. He's really Salix Peter, but everyone just calls him Pete or Peter G."

"Will I like him?"

"I expect do. People do. Like him better than me, mostly."

Pia swayed in and kissed him, and he stopped thinking of family and cuddled her close. She wasn't sticky any longer. He found himself thinking of delicious ways to please her, and he was about to suggest some of them when she reminded him that they were going to see her parents and sister.

Since Pia knew the way to her old home and he didn't, Peter disengaged his mind and went with her hand-in-hand through the pixie forest to one of the more distant villages. Pia drew him up to a low white cottage surrounded with flowers. She conjured the door open.

They stepped into a warm kitchen, where a pleasant-faced pixie man with brown hair and green eyes like Pia's was mending a worn-out pan. He looked up and smiled.

"Greet you, my dear. Are you and your friend going to be home for supper?" He regarded Peter in a friendly fashion.

Peter said, "No."

The man, presumably Pia's dad, focused on him. "Um . . . no? No what, master?"

"No, Pia and I won't be home for supper. At least, we will be, but not here."

Pia turned and gave him a look.

Peter added quickly, "Greet you, Master Tillien."

"Greet you, Master —" Pia's dad paused.

"Dad, this is my Peter," Pia said calmly.

The merry eyes passed over them. "I see. So, Pia's Peter, you and my daughter are having supper elsewhere?"

"Yes. We're going to be wed today."

"In that case, you should call me Gard." He stood up from the bench where he'd been working and came over to detach Peter from Pia's hand.

Peter hung on.

"You can let go. She won't go far." Gard Tillien addressed Pia. "Sweetheart, I think you'd better go and tell your mum what's happening. Don't worry about your Peter. He and I have things to talk over in private."

"Dad."

He gave her a sunny smile. "Off you go, my miss. The sooner you talk to your mother, the sooner Peter and I can get down to our little talk."

A few moments later, Peter was alone in the kitchen with Pia's dad. He bit his lip, uncertain of what to say and nervous about saying something wrong. In the event, Gard Tillien spoke first.

"Peter, when and how did you meet my daughter?"

Peter tried to think of a plausible story.

"You might as well tell me the truth. I can read you if you prefer."

"Fuck, no!"

"Or I might clap a compulsion on you."

"No!"

What if I babble about Barbie?

Tillien laughed. He had a good laugh, hearty and full, and his green eyes crinkled. "Stop looking so startled, my lad. Sit down." He gestured to a chair by the table and conjured tea things over with practised ease.

Peter sat down, but Tillien stayed standing, looking down

at him. "Am I making you uncomfortable, Pia's Peter?"

"Fuck, yes." Peter glowered at him.

"Good."

"Good? Fuck me, why would you want to do that?"

"Let me explain my position on this."

He has a fucking position?

Gard said mildly, "I'm a pixie father with two daughters who are the delight of my soul. I love their mother dearly, but my little misses . . . I made them. When they were born, I received them into my hands and kissed them. Mine were the first loving hands they ever knew. They are blood of my blood. If I thought anyone was stupid enough or careless enough to make one of them unhappy, then . . . well, I don't know what I'd do, but I assure you he wouldn't get a second chance. Their mother agrees with me in every particular. And I have some advice for you. Don't cross my miss. Not ever. If she likes you, she will love you as her son. If she doesn't, she will be exceedingly polite to you forever.

"That's my position and my miss's position upon Pia and Alba. Now you explain your position upon Pia."

Peter scowled as he put words to thoughts. "I met Pia in the pixie forest last night. I'm going to wed her. I will never let her be hurt if I can prevent it. Mine will be the most loving hands she will ever know . . . aside from family."

Gard Tillien took a step closer and conjured a plate of baked goods from the unseen larder. "Scone?"

Peter took one and bit into it. He ate it all and dusted flour off his fingers. It nearly choked him.

"Tea?"

Tillien pushed a cup towards him.

Peter drank it. Then he got to his feet, noting with satisfaction that he was taller than Pia's father. He hoped Gard had finished putting his position.

He hadn't.

"What have you been doing with my Pia since you met

her?" Tillien asked.

Peter wanted to growl that she was his Pia, but he restrained himself.

"That's our business. Pia's and mine. If she wants to tell you anything more about what we said and did when we met and since, she can. You're her dad, and she loves you. I'll tell you anything you like about me, but I won't tell you Pia's and my private business. I won't tell it to anyone." He thought of Pia snuggled in his arms, weeping a little, but holding on to him.

It'll be better next time. It's got to be. If not, we won't do it again. We'll have friendlies like the first one.

Gard Tillien hooked a second chair across to the table with one foot and folded himself down onto it. Then he smiled at Peter. "Good man."

Peter stared back.

Tillien said, "That was unkind of me, but when you and Pia have children I expect you'll do something similar, especially if one of them presents you with a miss or a man you've never heard of before but who has come to mean more to them than you do. What's your last name, lad?"

"Grene," Pia said, coming into the room arm in arm with a woman who must be her mother. "Mum, this is my Peter. Peter, this is my mum, Esther. Everyone calls her Tess."

Tess Tillien, an older and more mercurial version of Pia, looked him over slowly. She glanced at her husband.

"Gard?"

He turned out his hands.

Tess returned her regard to Peter. "Can he smile?" she asked Pia.

"Of course, he can."

Peter demonstrated, seeking evidence of the freezing politeness that would consign him to misery.

Tess said, "Hm." Then she bounced across the room and hugged him, almost knocking him backwards.

Peter closed his arms around her automatically. It felt odd. She was Pia's twin two decades on, but she wasn't his to hug. His gaze flicked anxiously to Master Tillien, whose green eyes had widened. Menace shone out of them for a few seconds before it was shuttered and tucked away.

He's had to learn that.

Mistress Tillien expelled her breath in a puff of surprise. "Glory, you're strong, lad. I bet you have a lovely grip on you." She leaned into his shoulder, drew in a noisy draught of air and reached up to kiss his cheek. "Greet you, my son. You can let me go now, before Gard says something unseemly and I have to discipline him. He'd enjoy it, the rogue, but it's not something I care to do before an audience."

Peter let go in a hurry.

Pia's mother blew out her cheeks expressively. "He's a good hugger," she said to her husband. "Smells good, too."

"Glad to hear it. Now come here to a real man who needs disciplining right now." He patted his knee invitingly.

Mistress Tillien spun over and settled on his lap, wrapping one arm around his neck. She winked at Peter and mouthed something he thought might have been *It's all right, dear.*

"Do I have to smack you, Gard?" she said aloud.

"No, darling. I'll behave." He bent and whispered something in her ear, and Tess Tillien blushed and laughed.

Pia put her hands on her hips and shook her head. "You're all as mad as bogles," she said. "Peter, did Dad give you afternoon tea, or has he been trying to intimidate you?"

"Both," Peter said.

"Good. I thought he might have skipped the tea."

"So, Master Grene, you and Pia are to be wed," Mistress Tillien said, looking at him kindly.

Peter said, "Yes, but my name's not Grene."

The three Tilliens gazed at him with identical surprise.

"Why does Pia think it is then?" Tillien asked.

"One of my grandfathers is called Grene. Master Berryman

Grene. He's a fucking vicar, but not a bad old bloke. People love him. The other one is Alexis Peckerdale. He's not a vicar. He knows things. Granny Jewel loves him . . . I think."

Comprehension dawned in Mistress Tillien's gaze. "If your name is Peckerdale and your grandfather is Master Alexis Peckerdale, you must be Jessie Grene's son! How lovely!" She turned to Pia. "Jessie and I were chums when we were kiddies, and we were sponsored together. Used to go to jazz clubs *over there*, but then she wed Gareth Peckerdale, and I wed Gard, and we got busy. Must catch up with her."

"Jessie?" Pia said uncertainly. Then she asked, "Peckerdale? Really?"

"Mum's called Jestima, and yes, Peckerdale. Really."

"So, I'll be Pia Peckerdale. Peter and Pia Peckerdale. Great bogle, Peter! We are not going to give our children P-names."

"There are plenty of names that don't start with P," he said. He thought privately there might not be any children after all. Trying to stuff a carrot into a radish skin was painful for both of them. He held out his arms. "Pia, please?"

She went to him and snuggled into his embrace. He went to pat her bottom, caught her mother's twinkling gaze, and did it anyway. Barbie had pulled away when he did that. Pia gave a pleased little wriggle and kissed his neck. He felt whole again. His miss liked his affection.

Then he said, "Thank you for the scone, Master Tillien, and for the kiss, Mistress Tillien. Pia and I are going to see my grandfather now to be wed. You can come if you like."

Master Tillien opened his mouth, and Mistress Tillien put her hand over it. "If you can bear to wait until tomorrow, I can refurbish my wedding dress for Pia to wear. It was my mother's and her mother's, going well back. It's charmed for joy."

Peter was about to say no when he felt Pia's quick turn of the head. He said, "Fuck it, if Pia wants to wear that wedding dress, I want her to do it, too. We'll arrange it with Grandad tonight and do it tomorrow."

Chapter Seven: At the Manse

The Manse, the Pixie Forest. September 1950
Peter Peckerdale

Peter was glad he'd agreed to postpone the wedding until the next day because when he visited his grandfather, the Reverend Berryman Grene delivered an unexpected and unwelcome response to his excited request.

"Don't be ridiculous, Peter. You cannot wed your miss on the day you met her."

"I met her yesterday, and I'm marrying her tomorrow, which makes three days," Peter growled. He clenched his hands in the pockets of his pixie pants. It felt strange not to have Pia's hand in his, but she and her ebullient mother had gone to visit his mother, Jestima. He wasn't too clear on why, and in any case, he was more interested in arguing with his grandfather.

"I am fucking well going to wed her. We're wish matched," he said.

"Then she'll wait for you."

"We don't want to wait. There's no reason to wait! We both have enough years." He flashed on his bliss when Pia was giving him their first friendly. She'd let him go first. She'd offered it. She'd loved the taste of him.

"Peter." His grandfather laid a hand on his shoulder.

Peter shook him off.

"Peter."

"What?"

"There is a good reason for you to wait, my son, and if you clear your mind of all that resentment, I'm sure you'll know what it is."

He said nothing, and after a minute or so, his grandfather kissed his brow. "I'll go out for a while and let you think."

Peter sat down suddenly in one of the wingchairs in his grandfather's study and propped his chin in his hands. He stared angrily at the wall. He was of age. No parent or grandparent had the power to prevent him from doing what he wanted. He could go through the gateway and never come back. He could *live human*. He squirmed, remembering Barbie's expression when he'd asked her for a friendly fuck. She'd agreed, finally, but she'd made him wear a rubber she'd got from Judit, and she wouldn't let him taste her.

It had been fun when they first met. Dating had been fun. Barbie loved dancing, and she had an open-eyed outlook on life. She'd accepted Peter's disclosure that he was fay and admitted she knew a few elf families in her hometown in New South Wales. She'd introduced him to her brother, Johnny, whom she categorised as a good egg. Johnny was, even though he'd wanted to play with Peter's blood.

Something brushed against Peter's leg, and he stopped thinking of Barbie and looked down into the amber eyes of a young red cat.

"Greet you, Red," he said shortly.

The cat chirruped and rubbed its furry cheek against his pants leg.

Peter quelled the desire to jerk away. He quite liked cats, although he liked goats a whole lot better, but this cat wasn't exactly or always a cat, and he wasn't comfortable with anyone rubbing against him without a good reason.

Except for Pia. She can rub herself wherever she likes . . . Ooh.

His balls had crinkled, startling him. He swallowed.

"If you've come to preach at me, you can do it in man form, and you'd better have your fucking pants on this time," he said.

The cat chirruped again, crouched, and unfolded into a boy of sixteen or so. Rory Inkersoll had red hair and amber eyes in both his forms. He was Berryman's ward as well as his apprentice in the vicarial business.

"Greet you, Rory." Peter nodded to him.

"I managed the pants and a tunic, too," Rory said, sitting opposite him in the second wingchair.

"I should fucking well hope so." Peter eyed the boy apprehensively. "That cat mani of yours was trying to read me. Bloody cheek."

"He does that. Don't worry about it. He won't judge you."

"You might."

"It's not my place to judge anyone but myself, Master Peckerdale. I leave that to the Lord."

"Good. You do that. I bet your Lord has his hands full, especially with us pixies. And next time you're talking to him ask him why a poor old geezer I knew had no one but me to hold his hand as he went to glory."

"That's simple. You were the best and kindest person available to see him on his way. Did he go easily?"

Peter thought back to sitting on a hard chair next to a white bed. Johnny had let him in, and Thadd had been pleased. He'd reached out, and Peter had taken his hand and then moved closer to give him a hug and some warmth. It hadn't been enough to bring him out of his latest crisis, but Peter had stayed there, holding on.

"I felt him go."

"Then he went from your kind hands directly to the Lord."

"I'm not fucking kind."

"Why were you with the old man then?"

He shrugged. "There was no one else. No friends. And now that dratted priest won't marry me to my miss."

Rory said, "If you're talking about Master Grene, I doubt if you should call him a dratted priest. He's your grandad."

"He's a pain in the bloody neck."

"Maybe all grandparents are. I wouldn't know."

"I s'pose not." Peter deflated. Rory's mother and her parents were all dead, and he didn't know his father.

"Maybe Master Grene thinks you should consider prayerfully before you wed a human maid," Rory suggested.

Peter stared at him. "What the fuck are you talking about? My Pia's a pixie miss."

"But you were living with a human maid in Appledore . . ." Rory sounded just slightly disapproving, which Peter thought a bit much considering the amount of time he reputedly spent with Mistress Emer Drumwiddy since her return from Erin a' Fee. Peter didn't know Mistress Drumwiddy, but he had heard she and Rory were good friends. They didn't live together, exactly . . .

Come to think of it, what do they do, exactly? I know he looked after her cottage while she was gone, the way Peter G did for Mum and me.

"I'm not living with her now! She left me," Peter snapped.

"I'd hope one of you had left if you're wedding a pixie miss. Your miss wouldn't stand for you living with another maid." The amber eyes contemplated him, and Rory added, "But it was only a few weeks ago you were here and talking about your human woman. When did you meet your new miss?"

"Last night," Peter growled.

"I see."

"And if you fucking well think I can't want her after lying down with her just the twice—" He broke off, feeling a blush surge up from his chest. He wasn't sure of Rory's age, but he knew he didn't have enough years to lie down with anyone. "Sorry."

The younger man gave him a sudden friendly grin. "Of course, I don't think that. If you've found the maid you want to love your whole life, of course, you know it. Love is one of the great mysteries and one of the great rewards. It's the Lord's great gift to us."

"Is that in the good book?" Peter asked suspiciously.

"Not in those terms, but that's what's meant. What's she like, your Mistress Pia?"

"She says what she thinks. She doesn't stand for any nonsense. She told me to persevere when things got a bit—awkward. I just want her to be happy forever."

"And you want to hold her close and tell her everything and have her love you because you're her man and not some wee scrap she took pity on?"

"Yes. That's it. How did you know? I hope that fucking cat of yours wasn't prowling about."

"He wasn't, but I know anyway. For one thing, you answered my question that way instead of mentioning her beautiful eyes and her beguiling curves."

"What do you know about her eyes and curves?" Peter growled.

"Not a thing, but I can't imagine you loving an ill-favoured lady."

Peter frowned and asked abruptly, "Could you?"

"I don't know. Maybe the one you love is always beautiful in your eyes. That's the way it goes."

"So, you understand. Why doesn't that dratted—I mean Grandad—see it?"

"I expect he wants to make sure you didn't just run to the nearest kind miss when you and your human maid fell out of love."

"I didn't. I wished. Anyway, we didn't fall out—Barbie and me. I was—fond of her. Still am. We just couldn't manage me being a pixie and her being human. There are things I need to do that she couldn't fucking well—sorry."

Rory got up and put his hand on Peter's slumped shoulder.

"You probably don't want my advice."

"Give it to me. You're going to be a fucking vicar. It's your job to advise."

"Maybe you could ask Master Grene when he would feel right about wedding you to your miss. It's not as if you can't lie down with her and love her until then. You've done it already, and it can't be a sin if it's done in love and does no harm to anyone."

"But what if some other green-willied fucker gets her—"

Rory looked taken aback. "Peter, if you think your miss could be got, then you should certainly not wed her, ever."

"I don't think it. I just feel it. I want her so much that I think every man must feel the same way. Fuck it. You'd want her if you had enough years to want anyone that way."

"Pixie misses are lovely, but I've chosen someone else."

"Who?"

"I won't tell you. I haven't told her yet. It's not appropriate."

"Fuck me! What's appropriate got to do with it?"

"Quite a lot. I don't have enough years, and she has plenty. If you fear someone might want your Pia over the next few weeks, spare a thought for me. I've got more than a year to worry and wait!"

Peter saw his hands clench. "I'm sorry, man," he said with a rush. Then he said, "But she'll wait for you."

"I pray so every day." Rory ran a hand through his rumpled red hair. "Anyway, Master Peckerdale, if your miss has given herself to you that way and still wants you after it, then she's made her choice. Will you answer a question for me?"

"I might if it's not too fucking personal."

"It's very personal, but it means a lot to me to know."

"Go on then. Ask."

Rory's cheeks reddened, clashing with his hair. His amber eyes brimmed with unshed tears. "Peter, when you—when you and she had lain together and that — it — was over, what did she do?"

Peter felt his own face blushing.

"You're going green," Rory observed.

"Yes. We pixies fucking well do that when we're embarrassed. But since you asked . . . She snuggled up against me, close to me as she could get." He sniffed and blinked back sudden threatening tears. "Fuck it. Now you've got me crying like a maid!"

"And you? How did you feel?"

"Like the most fortunate man ever born. I'll do anything to make her happy."

"Thank you. I pray to feel the same way when my turn comes."

The young man folded in on himself and became the red cat again. He strolled over to the door and melted through it.

Peter shook his head. *Damn. How does he do that?*

CHAPTER EIGHT: THE JOY RING

The Manse, the Pixie Forest. September 1950
Peter Peckerdale

Peter was still pondering when his grandfather came back into the room.

"Well, grandson? Have you come to an understanding?"

"Yes, you old bugger. You think it's all too quick, and it might not be real, and so you won't say the words for us."

"I won't say them yet. I couldn't do it, Peter. Not in good conscience."

"What about your hob-knob friend?"

"If you're talking about Master Charming, you'd have to ask him. He might do it, since he doesn't know the circumstances with your human maid."

Peter scowled. "I want you to do it. 'Cause you're family. If we wait for a few weeks, would you do it then?"

"That depends." His grandfather held up a hand. "I'm not trying to be difficult. I very much want to see you and Peter G settled happily with loving companions. I just want to be sure you lads wed your true forevers and don't just make do with a warm miss for your beds."

Peter was slightly diverted by the idea of Peter G wedding anyone. He remembered he hadn't seen much of him for a few weeks . . . not since he'd gone *over there* to live in Lady Lydia Appledore House and do some work in the human world. He'd left Peter G in nominal charge of his goats and the cottage. He'd been back a few times, but never for long. He'd had to be *over there* when someone wanted to draw him, and then there was Barbie.

"Pete's not courting, is he?" he said, only half-joking.

"Peter G is a child," his grandfather reminded him.

"Yes, but —" Peter tried to explain his view that his cousin Salix Peter Grene, who preferred to be called by his second name, wasn't really a child. He was just a wise and sensible person who happened to be six years old. As usual, his grandfather failed to see his point, so he switched the conversation. "Has he been minding my goats?"

"Assiduously," Berryman Grene assured him so drily that Peter gathered his cousin had been spending a great deal of time in caprine company.

"He might be at the cottage when Pia and I go there tonight, then."

"Most likely. If so, you might tell him Russet would like to see him sooner rather than later. She feels responsible for raising him and that she's failing in her duty."

"She can't raise Peter G. He's already raised. He was born raised." Peter thought back to his twelve-year-old self when Aunt Russet, resting in one of Grandad's wingback chairs with a swaddled bundle in her arms, had looked up at him when he entered the study.

The Manse. Summer 1944.

"Peter, love, meet Salix Peter. I hope you'll be good friends."

Peter doubted it, since he was twelve and Salix Peter was a newborn baby, but he agreed politely.

"Would you like to hold him?" Aunt Russet asked.

No.

But she offered the bundle in the clear expectation that he would, so he held out his hands and accepted wordlessly. He juggled the bundle around to find the top end and inspected the small face. The baby was awake, and Peter perceived he had reddish-brown hair like Aunt Russet's and big wondering eyes.

"You've got him wrapped too tightly." He loosened the blanket, and two small arms waved free. "That's better." He examined the child, and the baby stared solemnly back, relaxed and attentive. "He likes me."

"I thought he might," Aunt Russet said. "Quercus and I hope you don't mind sharing your name with your cousin. We put a Salix in front of it, but he just seems like a Peter."

"I'm happy to share it, and anyhow, Great-grandad Grene had it first. I can be Peter P, and he can be Peter G. Pete. Greet you, Pete!" He bounced the baby gently, and the little boy went on looking into his eyes. "Hey, the little bugger's reading me!"

"He does that. Gets it from me."

"You mean you read me?"

"Of course, I read you, Peter! You don't think I'd hand my baby over to just anyone to hold, do you?"

"How would I know?"

"I assure you I take due care. Aside from Quercus, Berry and my dad, you're the first pixie man to hold him. We hope you'll be his godfather."

"Who, me? Shit, Aunt Russet, I'm not holy enough!"

"Darling Peter, you don't have to be holy. You have to be trustworthy, and you have to be willing to care for his happiness — always. You also have to be strong enough to tell him if you see him making a bad choice. Think you can do that?"

"I'll fucking well try." Peter hugged the baby, who turned its face to his chest. "Look here, Peter G, you're making a bad choice there. I don't have tits, so I can't give you milk. You need a pixie miss for that. Lucky for you, there's one right here." He glanced at his aunt.

She rolled her eyes. "You'll do. Hand him over, and I'll feed him. And you run along. You're not watching this."

"Why not? It'll be interesting. I've seen goats giving suck, but they do it standing up."

"No doubt, but you're too old and too young to watch this, and your uncle wouldn't like it. Now, go."

Peter handed over the baby and went, whistling to himself. He'd seen plenty of tree maids feeding their babies. It wasn't polite to stare, but they didn't mind if he stopped for a chat while they were doing it. Tree maids were always kind and friendly, as long as he stood at a respectful distance. He didn't know how they judged it, but they never got it wrong.

The Manse. September 1950

Peter came out of his memories with a rush. "What did you say, Grandad?"

"I was telling you Peter G's mother wants him to come home."

"I'll tell him then. Grandad, did you send Rory Inkersoll to preach at me?"

"I did not. I left you to think alone."

"Oh. He came, anyway. Odd fellow, isn't he?"

"He's unusual, but he'll make a good priest."

"If his parishioners get stroppy, he can fucking well claw them into submission."

"Language, Peter."

Peter said reflectively, "That's what my miss says."

"And do you take notice?"

"I take notice of everything she says because she might be offering me a friendly." He sighed. "I don't see why we need to wait. You know wish matches work. Have you ever known one that didn't?"

"Yes."

The single syllable startled Peter.

Berryman looked troubled. "It depends on the wording

and the intention of the wish. If a person who isn't compatible tries to service a wish out of kindness, or curiosity or lust — no matter how well-intentioned — then the match will eventually go bad. Some wish matches even have built-in limitations. I knew a maid who was open-hearted, sweet, kind, and appealing. She made a wish for a loving man, but there was no cuddle into the future thought."

"How the fuck did that work?"

"I don't know the details, but I do know she had a short time of happiness. The eventual result was good, but it wasn't what most folk want from a wish match. That's why I don't encourage them."

Peter cocked an eyebrow. "You're not wished with Granny Clover?"

"Well . . . I love her dearly, and she loves me, but we decided neither of us would put a wish in it."

Peter knew a prevarication when he heard one. He stared hard at his grandfather. "You're fucking evading me."

Berryman had the grace to look ashamed. Then his lips tipped up at the corners. "You're right. What I said was true, but when I got her emerald ring from Master Pendennis . . . that's Jago's grandfather, Tintagel . . . I charmed it and inadvertently wished her joy.

"She said I was her joy, and we both realised what had happened."

"So, you're wish matched."

"In the manner of speaking. I was afraid for a while that the ring itself was the source of the joy, but then when your mother settled on Gareth for her forever, Clover lent the ring to her for a while."

"What the fuck for?"

"Generosity, or maybe as an experiment. Your grandmother is a wise woman, and she knew I was nervous about it."

"So, what happened?"

"Clover assured me she felt just as much joy as before, and Jessie is equally happy with your father."

"And Granny Clover got the ring back?"

Berryman said, "Yes. Then Russet wore it for a time. It's become a family tradition. Would you like your miss to have it until you wed?"

Peter clutched at that question. "So, you will wed us?"

"In due time. But let's get back to the wish match. As I said, I don't encourage them, but it seems a great many of us wish anyway."

"Well, I did, and Pia did."

He reflected on the wording of his wish. He hadn't been specifically wishing for a miss to wed . . . he'd just wanted the pain to stop. He prodded the thought of Barbie.

Hope you're well, my girl.

He touched the thought of Pia.

Mine. Forever.

"What's done is done," Berryman said.

"I wouldn't undo it for the world." He bit his lip. "Fuck it, Grandad! I want you to be the one to say the words, so I'll see if Pia agrees to spend a few weeks as lovies before we're wed."

"What if she doesn't agree?" his grandfather asked.

"Then we'll ask the fucking hob-knob man to say the words. I think she'll want you, though. By the way, you said that maid's wish match had a good result in the end. What did you mean?"

"Forget it. I shouldn't have mentioned it."

"What was the result?"

His grandfather gave a sharp sigh. "Peter, you are the most aggravating pixie man I know, and I know a lot of pixie men. The result was Rory. No, I won't tell you more. It's not your business., but I think most folk would agree that a world with Rory Inkersoll in it is better than a world without."

"His fucking cat mani read me."

"Rory's cat self is the least of your worries if you wed in haste."

A piece of paper landed on Berryman's lap, and he picked it up. "This conversation, interesting though it is, needs to end. Your grandmother says we have callers."

"I'll go, then."

"You should stay. They're coming in, and it will look discourteous if you dash off."

Peter glanced at the door with alarm, not wanting to be polite to any visiting parishioners. He was half on his feet when Berryman called, "Come in," and the door swung open.

Berry clicked his fingers, and five more chairs appeared, crowding the study.

Peter sat down in a hurry.

"Greet you, my friends. My dear." Berry got up and kissed his miss, Clover. He offered his hand to Mistress Tillien, then to her husband, then to Pia. Finally, he held out both hands to his daughter, Jestima, and son-by-love, Gareth Peckerdale.

"Sit down, everyone," he added.

Peter did a quick computation. Granny, Mum and Dad, Pia and her mum and dad. He realised they had one chair too few for the company. He half got up again, indicating that his grandmother should take his chair.

Clover waved him away, the emerald ring twinkling on her hand. "Don't start bouncing about, Peter." She asked the others to sit and beckoned to Pia. "I expect you'd like to sit on Peter, my dear. It might keep him in one place for more than five seconds."

Pia, blushing, came over to him and he held out his arms and took her gratefully onto his lap. He relaxed as she settled against him.

That's better.

He slipped a hand under her tunic and rested it on her bare waist.

"About tomorrow," he said softly.

Pia leaned back and looked up at him. "Would you mind very much if we wait a bit longer? Mum wants to add a breadth to the wedding dress because I'm taller than she is, and we need to get rings from Master Pendennis, and I'd like Alba to be my bridesmaiden. If you mind, we can forget that, though."

Peter smiled at her. "We'll have to wait a bit. Grandad won't do it yet."

"Because of Barbie?" she whispered.

"How'd you know?"

"It just seemed likely. He didn't say he wouldn't do it at all?"

"No-o. He said—no, I said—a few weeks. Is that all right?"

"Of course." She put her face to his, and he kissed her.

When he looked up, Clover Grene had got to her feet and was looking down at them. She addressed herself to Pia. "My dear, Berry informs me you and my flighty grandson are wish matched. Therefore, I'd love to offer you this ring to wear for a while. It was made by Master Tintagel Pendennis years ago and charmed by the very best man I know. Would you like to borrow it?"

Pia glanced at Peter as if asking permission.

He wanted to give her a special ring, just for her, but that could wait until their wedding.

The sooner I can get any ring on her finger . . .

He said, "That's a fucking grand idea if you'd like to."

Pia's eyes lit up, and Clover slid the ring from her finger, kissed it, and passed it to Peter.

"Cast a glamour, Peter. We don't need to hear what words you choose to say."

Peter glanced at her with gratitude and cast the glamour. The sound faded, and he saw a luminous pale light enclose them.

That's fucking weird.

He almost panicked, but Pia was with him, so he took a firm grasp of her hand. He was about to put the ring on her finger when he had an idea and laid it in her palm instead.

"Pia, this is Granny's ring, and it says you're going to wed me soon. I'm fucking well going to get you a perfect ring just for you for the wedding, but this one's a promise for now. I'll put the wedding ring on your finger, but this one . . . I want you to put it on for yourself." He swallowed. "But only, only, if you want this as much as I do. Won't be able to bear it if you don't, but it'd be fucking worse if you did it just for kindness."

Pia said, "You numpty! It's not just for kindness. You're mine, my forever." She put on the ring.

The study and the buzz of talk eased back as the glamour faded, but Peter was aware only of the warmth of his forever in his arms.

A door opened.

"Peter."

Go away.

"Peter."

I'm busy.

"Peter!"

Still holding Pia close, he turned his face to snap, "What?"

"I might ask you the same thing. What, by the original forest, are you doing with that miss?"

Peter blinked, trying to focus. "Greet you, Grandad. Greet you, Granny."

Pia whispered, "Grandad?"

"This is the other one, the not-vicar." Carefully, he slid his hands out from under Pia's tunic and ostentatiously wrapped his arms around her clothed shoulders. He got up from the chair, steadying her on her feet. "Pia, these are my Peckerdale grandparents, Alexis and Jewel. Granny, Grandad, this is my Pia. If you two would like to share this chair, we're just going."

"Peter!" That was his mother, and he tossed her a

reassuring glance.

"It's all right, Mum . . . Pia and I need to go to the cottage and arrange a few things. We want to live there for a while, if that's not a problem?" he added belatedly.

"That's not a problem, darling." Jestima got up. She embraced Jewel Peckerdale and bobbed a playful curtsey to Alexis and then came over to hug Peter. Since he was still holding Pia, Pia ended up as the filling in a hug sandwich, but she didn't seem to mind.

Jestima whispered, "You two scamper off and have a lovely time. Don't worry about anything. We'll all have a good gossip and some afternoon tea. Then if you like, we can help you plan your wedding in a few weeks. Does that sound sensible?"

"Fucking marvellous," Peter said distractedly. He detached himself and Pia and got them out of the study. His grandfather Peckerdale yelled after him, "If you see your cousin Salix, send him home to his mother!"

"We will," Peter yelled back.

CHAPTER NINE: THE COTTAGE

The Cottage, the Pixie Forest. September 1950
Peter Peckerdale

Peter left the manse hand-in-hand with Pia, and he said, "Hope you don't mind us leaving, but it was fucking crowded in there."

Pia looked slightly dazed, but she smiled. "I'm glad. They all seemed lovely."

Peter snorted. "Granny Jewel's lovely. Grandad Alexis is not lovely. Cranky old geezer, argue the hind leg off a billy-goat."

"He looks exactly like you, except for the eyes."

"I know. Why d'you think I got you out of there? Once Grandad Alexis gets going, no one else can get a word in, and you might have run for the hills in case I turned out like him."

"I won't. I know what you're like already."

"Mind, he's fucking clever about stuff. He knows people *over there* who can do things with banks and shares. He got Prue to find me a place to live for a while."

"Who's Prue?"

"Prue Leilana, she was, but she's wed to a halfling. Halfling herself, come to that. Kind of a cousin of Grandma Jewel's. Why?"

Pia said, "I wondered if she was another maid you'd loved."

He squeezed her hand and stopped to kiss her. "No, she's a down-the-line cousin. You're the maid I love."

She clung to him. "Forever?"

"Forever. Always."

Pia sighed and moved back a step. "Good. Are we going to your mum's cottage now?"

"Yes." He disengaged his mind from the journey and concentrated on holding Pia's hand. "It's a bit out of the way," he said.

"I don't mind."

For all his faith in his cousin Peter G, Peter was a little doubtful of how the cottage would appear to Pia. It was small and functional, but since no one had lived there full time in nearly twenty years, it lacked all but the most basic furnishings.

The sun was setting as they arrived, and he was pleased to note the garden was still producing well. As they closed in on the gate in the low white fence, a loud bleat gave him just enough time to warn Pia to stand aside. She moved to the fence as a wave of brindled fay goats converged on him.

Peter laughed. He felt ridiculously pleased to see them again and crouched with his arms outstretched so his friends could nibble at his hands and shoulders without knocking him over. He conjured gingerbread from the crock in the cottage and broke it for them. After a couple of minutes, the goats had finished expressing their opinion of his absence. Snick, the biggest of the billies, was inclined to grumble and flourish his horns, but Peter mollified him with an extra treat.

"You were all right with Pete, you old bugger . . . Shoo now," he said, and the goats hustled off. Grinning, he turned back to Pia, saying, "I'll introduce you in the morning—" He broke off when he saw Pia in conversation with his cousin.

"Peter G!" He bounced to his feet and strode up to meet him. "You've grown."

"You haven't," the boy retorted.

"I don't need to. Quite big enough."

Too big in one way.

"Are we having supper soon?"

Peter was about to say of course they were when he remembered his miss. "Er—" he turned to look at her, and a great gush of delight ran through him. "Peter G, this is my miss, my Pia."

"I know. She told me. That's why I asked about supper. Pia says Mum wants me home, so if we're going to eat, it's got to be soon."

Peter was still watching Pia. It had suddenly struck him that she might think it peculiar if they shared their first supper together with a six-year-old boy . . . or maybe seven? To his relief, she seemed amused. "Pia?" he said

"I should think we could eat soon if there's anything to have," she said.

"Is there?" Peter asked.

"Plenty," Peter G informed them. He indicated the garden. "I fixed wards to keep the goats out. Snick is cranky with me, but I thought you'd be cranky if he ate all your peas."

"Hey, you can do wards already. Fuck it. I couldn't do that till I was eleven or so."

"I can do wards. Can't conjure yet."

"Supper, then," Peter said. He took Pia's hand and led her into the garden.

Peter G darted ahead and opened the door. "You've got to pick her up and carry her in," he instructed.

"Why?"

"Gentie says that's what pixie men do for their lovies. And Pia's your lovie, so you've got to make sure she doesn't trip on the step."

"Good idea." Peter scooped Pia off her feet and carried her in. He wanted to put her on the bed and get down to some forevering, but Peter G was watching them with interest, so he stood her in the little kitchen instead. "Welcome home, Pia."

"Thank you." She kissed his cheek and looked about. "Have you been sleeping here, sweetie?" she asked Peter G.

He shook his head, regretfully. "Mum wants me home by dark. She says the bogles will get me if I stay out late."

"That's fucking nonsense," Peter said.

Peter G said, "Gentie says there are bogles in the alplands."

"Who's Gentie?"

"You know. She's my . . ." The child paused. "She's my friend."

"Oh?" Peter felt a stir of indulgent curiosity. He remembered hearing the name before, but he couldn't bring a face to mind. "Where did you meet her?" He opened the larder and was pleased to see it well stocked. He flicked his fingers to light the lamps, as it was growing dim inside the cottage.

Peter G poked up the range, added some small pieces of wood, and pushed the kettle into place. "Haven't met her yet. I'm going to have to find her, but not for a while. Mum and Dad won't let me."

"Bugger!" Peter said with sympathy. "How do you know what she thinks about bogles then?"

"She's got the sight. She likes making soup. Her granny teaches her."

"Maybe she'll make soup for you when you find her."

"She will. She's going to teach me how." Peter G reached past Peter and took a loaf of bread from the larder. He handed it to Pia. "There's butter in the crock, Mistress Pia. I got it from one of the dairy hobs. There's goat cheese in that jar. I poured olive oil on it and put in some pepper. Gentie says that keeps it good."

"Gentie must be a sensible person," Pia said, and she began preparing bread and cheese.

The kettle boiled, and Peter poured tea into three cups while Peter G carefully cut the tops off radishes and tomatoes.

They sat companionably around the table and ate, but

Peter G soon got down. "Got to go now, or Mum will come looking for me."

"Because of the bogles?" Pia asked.

"No, because I'm not home when she expects me. The bogles won't hurt me. Gentie says gingerbread will calm them, so I'm taking some with me."

Peter rose, too. "Thanks for looking after things here, Pete."

"That's all right. Are you going to be here always now, or are you going *over there* again to stay?"

"We're going to be here."

"Right. You won't need me, then." He paused, looking uncertain, and then said with a rush, "Can I still come over, or do you want to be private with Pia?"

"Um—" Peter did very much want to be private with Pia, but he was aware of being on shaky ground. His cousin had looked after things splendidly.

Pia came to his rescue. "We'd love to see you tomorrow, but maybe after our dinner? We can have a picnic for afternoon tea, and you can tell me some more about your friend. That's if you'd like to?"

Peter G grinned, showing a missing tooth. "Can we go to the falls? Mum doesn't like me going there on my own."

"You just want to look at the bare water maids," Peter said.

The child looked exasperated. "He's being silly. Water maids are lovely, but I'm not interested in whether they're bare or not," he told Pia. "I like to swim. Hula's going to show me how to go under the falls, but she says I have to have a grown-up with me to give permission. She also says not to let Lia take me because Lia sometimes forgets folk don't all have water-lungs."

"You'd better scoot for home," Peter said. He had a sudden vision of Aunt Russet sweeping vengefully into the cottage looking for her son. Words would be said, and he'd had quite enough of being scolded like an errant child.

72

"I'm going now. I'll come back tomorrow after dinner. I'll knock on the door in case you're busy with something private."

Peter held out his hand, and his cousin shook it gravely. Then the boy turned to Pia. "Goodnight, Mistress Pia. It's been lovely to meet you. May I kiss you goodbye, or will that make Peter cranky?"

"You may certainly kiss me goodbye if you'd like to. Peter will not be cranky if I share a hug with a friend," Pia said. She was still seated, so Peter G leaned over and put an arm around her neck while he kissed her cheek.

"You smell nice," he said. Then he darted for the door and was gone.

Peter said, "I'm sorry about that, but he has been looking after the goats, so I couldn't just tell him to fucking well leave."

To his relief, Pia smiled. "So that's your friend Peter G. He's a sweetie."

"Got better manners than I have," Peter said regretfully.

"Yes. It must be difficult to be as old in your head and as young in your body as he is."

"I expect it is."

"He's lucky he has you as a friend as well as a cousin."

"What? Why?" Peter forbore to tell her he was Peter G's godfather. Time enough for that.

Pia shrugged. "I'm not sure why I think that. I just do. I hope I can be his friend, too, because he seems a bit lonely." She looked up at him. "Peter, do you think we could wash the crocks tomorrow instead of doing them now?"

"Yes." He felt a catch of excitement. "Are you ready for bed?"

"Yes, I am. I want to hold on to you and sleep."

He took her hand and led her wordlessly into the small bedroom. "I have to make up the bed. The privy's out the back, if you need to go."

She thanked him and went out. Peter's hands were shaking too much to conjure, so he took linen sheets from the chest and made up the springyweed mattress. There was a quilt his mother had made when she lived in the cottage before wedding his father, and a braeside wool blanket he'd got in exchange for helping one of the shepherds with a busy lambing season the year before. He hoped it would do.

He thought about posing for Thadd, standing patiently in an odd position while the old man sketched, scraped, painted, scraped, cursed and bemoaned the shake in his hands.

"I don't shake if I drink, darling, but I need clarity," he'd said to Peter.

Close to the end of his work he'd put an arm around Peter and one around Judit and hugged them. "I've had scads of models in my misspent life, my darlings, but you're the best. Should have found you thirty years ago. Might have kept me from the drink."

"Even I wasn't born that long ago, Thaddie," Judit said.

The old man had let go and wandered back to the third panel of his work. "My life's not been wasted, in any event. I might be a scrawny old queer without blood of my own, but I've given beauty to the world."

Peter switched his mind away from a life so close to ending, to his own life, which felt as if it was about to begin.

Fuck it. Wish Thadd could have painted Pia. He'd have loved her.

He was still patting nervously at the quilt, which was stitched with flowers and leaves, when Pia came back. The soft wisps of hair around her face were damp, so he assumed she'd had a wash at the pump.

I'd better wash, too . . . in case . . .

"The bed's made up," he said unnecessarily.

"Are you going out?" she asked.

"Yes. To wash." He departed at speed.

When he returned, Pia was lying in bed with her hands behind her head.

He conjured off his clothing and got in beside her. "Pia . . ."

She rolled towards him and put her arms around him, pushing her face into his neck.

Peter felt a wave of possessive love roll over him. *My miss. Mine.* He tucked her closer.

They lay like that for a while, and Peter thought about all he wanted to say to her. There were plans to make and things to tell and to ask. She was quiet, though, so he said nothing. After a bit, he felt her hand close on his thumb. She was asleep.

Well . . . He rolled her over gently and used his free hand to take a generous handful of her breast. She hadn't minded that last night, and it felt so right. He kissed her bare shoulder and then her neck through the curtain of hair.

Mine. He hitched closer, so their bodies were in full contact. His willy made urgent propositions about having a friendly now, this instant.

No. She wants to sleep. You can wait until she's ready.

He concentrated on adjusting his grip to the pressure she'd wanted the night before. He relaxed and slept.

He woke, as he had the day before, in the early dawn. Pia was pressed against him, still holding his hand in a possessive grasp. He flexed his fingers. She squeezed back.

She's awake.

He kissed the back of her neck again. "Greet you, Pia."

"Greet you, Peter. Peter. I do like that name. I'm glad your parents chose it for you."

"Family name," he said.

"I need to go to the privy."

He laughed, breathlessly. "So do I. You go first, and I'll stoke up the stove. Watch out for goats."

"Peter G said he'd warded the garden."

"Fuck! So he did. Good. I wonder why I never thought of doing that?"

Pia let go of his hand and wriggled away. "Back soon," she said.

Peter watched her walk across the room, and his heart caught at how beautifully formed she was. She'd said looks didn't matter, but to him, they were part of the parcel.

He got out of bed and went into the kitchen to put wood on the stove. The pieces were small, and he realised Peter G must have cut them and carried them by hand.

He should be playing with scamps his own age.

Fuck, there's no one his own age. He's six, and he's also sixteen and possibly sixty. Maybe he ought to spend more time with the fucking cat man. They're both peculiar cusses.

He slid the kettle into place and put tea in the pot. Then he went to the privy.

Pia was standing by the pump, looking out over the first wash of sunlight in the garden. She seemed stiff and uneasy.

Peter used the privy and came to wash his face and hands. As he splashed, he said, "Pia? Are you all right?"

She glanced at his face and then down at his willy and looked away. "Yes, of course."

"There's no fucking of course about it. What's wrong?"

She said, still facing away, "I want to be yours."

"You are mine. My forever."

"I know. I mean, I want to be with you."

He touched her shoulder, finding it rigid. "Pia, come here."

She didn't turn, so he came up closer and put his arms around her from behind, rested his cheek on her head and hugged her.

She leaned into his embrace, and he felt all his senses coming alive.

"Do you feel like a friendly?" he ventured.

She stiffened.

Right. The last one hurt her.

"We can do it the way we did first. If you like." He swallowed and said in a rush, "We don't ever have to do the other way again."

She burst into tears and turned into his arms, wetting his shoulder.

"Pia, let's just go to bed and cuddle. That'd be fucking lovely."

She nodded against his chest.

Back in bed, she sniffled and said, "That was unpardonable of me to burden you with my silly fears."

He gave her a squeeze. "You fucking well go on telling me stuff. I can't know if you don't. I'm not good at reading people. I get things wrong."

"All right." She lifted her face and kissed him until they were both breathing heavily.

Peter broke off and gritted his teeth in discomfort.

Pia pushed her hand between them and grasped him, making him jump. "I want to try something."

"Anything. Only do it now. I'm bursting."

She moved down the bed. She'd been so assured that first time, but this morning he felt her hesitating. He patted her shoulder urgently, and she took an audible breath and clamped her mouth around him.

It was bliss. He lay soaking up the attention, trying to hold the moment. She shifted away, and he bit his tongue to keep from protesting as she came up to lie beside him.

She put her hand on his chest. "I think I'm ready now for you to get in me. I've made you wet and slippery."

"What about you?"

"I'm wet and slippery, too. Feel."

He slipped a hand down and felt. "I can make it better." He heaved up to his knees, bent and licked her lovingly, wetting her more with his tongue. Then he moved up between her upraised knees. "Stop me if it hurts too much. I mean it. Fucking stop me."

"Yes."

He kissed her and slid cautiously in. She was still tight, but after the first wince, he felt her exhale against his mouth. "Do you need to stop?"

"No. It's better. Put your hands under me."

He pushed his hands under her, lifting her to a slight angle. She murmured, "Now move."

Still cautiously, he did move, and he felt surfaces flexing and adjusting. She clutched at him, panting, and uttered a squeak. He felt the tight embrace on his willy squeezing rhythmically, and the sensation tipped him over the edge with a sigh.

Another pixie grip. Fucking lovely.

He went on moving gently, kissing her with loving attention until she turned her face away.

"Better?" he asked.

"Much." She rolled her head to look back at him. "Did you remember to hold?"

"I hope so." He couldn't remember, really.

Pia kissed him again. "You didn't say all the oh-fucks. Wasn't it as good this time?"

"Lovely. I loved it. Only I was thinking more about you and less about my willy. I'm going to pull out now, so relax."

"Don't. Just wait until it slips out on its own."

"Why?"

She mumbled, "Feels nice in me. Like kissing."

He wasn't sure what she meant, but being close like that felt right, so he went on supporting his weight on his elbows until nice became squishy and they had to roll apart to mop up.

"You're all damp," Peter observed, leaning his cheek on her brow.

"Mm. Can we stay here until dinner time?"

"What about breakfast?"

"Bread and butter?"

"And tea. I'll get up and get it."

She laughed and conjured a plate of bread and butter from the larder, but Peter did get up to make the tea. Conjuring boiling water about needed a lot of concentration, and he felt wrung out and pleasantly tired. He brought the tea back and got into bed, and he and Pia ate and drank and then enjoyed a brief nap before getting up to wash, eat a sketchy dinner and ready a picnic for their expedition with Peter G.

Chapter Ten: Wedding

The Pixie Forest. October 1950
Peter G

Peter G was so pleased and proud he had to tell somebody or burst.

He wanted to tell Gentie, but that would have to wait until she called for him again. He prowled about until his mother told him to go and find something useful to do.

"I'll bring in the wood."

"You do that, Pete." She kissed him affectionately and ruffled his hair. "When you've finished, go over to Grandad Grene at the manse."

"He said no lessons today." Grandad Grene was teaching him figuring. He could read and write already, but figures were his special delight. He loved the patterns they made.

"Not for lessons, unless Master Rory has time to help you. Mistress Hillyard is bringing a suit for you to try on."

Peter G didn't know Mistress Hillyard, but he was used to meeting new people. Because Grandad Grene was a vicar, he often had strangers coming to visit. He went out to the wood stack.

To his disappointment, he found that someone, probably his dad, had conjured the wood in already. The wood box was full. Peter decided to go to Grandad Grene's place anyway.

Everyone was busy there, too, but Rory Inkersoll was reading in a corner of the study.

"Greet you, Master Inkersoll." He didn't ask about the

lesson, because Rory looked as if his mind was somewhere else.

Rory stuck his finger in his book and looked up, his amber eyes shifting a little as they came into focus. "Master Grene. You're looking pleased with life."

"I am. Can I tell you something special?"

"Yes, as long as it's not something you shouldn't share with me."

"It's not like that. It's about Peter P and Mistress Pia, and not a private thing."

"They're being wed in a few days."

"Yes, but it's not just that. I like Pia," he added reflectively.

Rory gave his sudden quick smile. His red hair, far brighter than Peter G's own rusty thatch, shone in the sunlight fingering in from the window. "I'm glad you like Mistress Pia, lad."

"She's my friend."

"So instead of losing one friend to a new love, now you have two good friends where you had one before."

Peter G nodded. That was it exactly. "Mistress Pia likes having me around as long as it's not too often or for too long. They don't mind that I'm not as old as them. You have an older friend, too, haven't you?"

Rory's smile bloomed again, and he said, "That I have."

"So that's like Mistress Pia and me."

"No, lad. At least, I hope not, because that would be uncomfortable for both of you, and Peter P might go pixie on you."

"Go pixie?"

"Never mind." Rory jerked his thumb back and let the book snap shut. "What was the important thing you were going to tell me?"

Peter G wanted to hug himself, but that was a special thing he did only sometimes, so he didn't. He said, "Peter asked me to stand up with him when he marries Pia. I'm to make sure he doesn't forget the ring or say something he shouldn't and make the handover promise for him. I'm also to look after the joy ring."

Rory reached out a long-fingered hand and grasped Peter G's in friendship. "Splendid! You're the best choice there could ever be for that role." He looked over Peter G's shoulder and added, "There's a lady looking for one of us, I think."

Peter G disengaged his hand and turned unhurriedly to the door, where a tall young woman with fair hair stood watching them. She had a bundle of cloth over her arm, and she focused her gaze on Rory.

Peter G said, "Are you, Mistress Hillyard? Mum said you wanted to see me to fit my clothes for my cousin's wedding."

The woman looked surprised. "Are you Salix Grene, then? I thought—" She broke off as Rory Inkersoll laughed. "What?"

Rory said to Peter G, "I think Mistress Hillyard thought I was the man in question. I'd best leave you to it. I have somewhere else to be and someone I long to see." He winked at Peter G and folded down into his red cat form before padding over to the wall and phasing through it.

Mistress Hillyard stared after him and said, "Lawks a mercy! Who was that?"

Peter G stored that comment away for future use. He came forward and offered his hand to the woman. "Greet you, Mistress Hillyard. That was Master Rory Inkersoll. He's going to be a vicar."

"A cat is going to be a vicar?"

Peter G shook his head vigorously. "No, the red cat isn't going to be a vicar. Master Rory is. Don't let it trouble you."

She looked down at him, clearly amused. "I won't, then. I'll tell my sister-by-love about him, though, when I see her again. She'll be most interested, Master Salix."

The measuring and trying on took only a little time because

Mistress Hillyard had a fay talent for clothing. She offered Peter G three swatches of cloth to choose from and said he'd picked well. Soon after that, he was the owner of a smart suit of long pants with a button-up waistcoat over a big linen shirt with green embroidery.

Peter G surveyed himself in the looking glass. He wished Gentie could see him looking like this. Maybe next time she sent for him, he could wear his new clothes.

"The shirt's big," he said.

Mistress Hillyard put her head to one side, so her crown of fair hair shone in the light from the window. "Liebchen, I think I must have made that for the man-to-be. It has gathers and cuffs, so it can get bigger as you do. Do you like it? If not, I can make you one for the lad-you-are."

"I like it this way. It's dashing."

"I'm glad. I like folk to feel right in my clothes, even if they're a *kleines bisschen Zukunft*."

He must have looked puzzled because she laughed and said, "A small bit future." Then she offered her hand as if he'd been a man already and went to fit someone else.

The wedding happened three days later. It was a joyful occasion, but quite a lot of folk cried. Even Peter P cried a bit, but that seemed to be all right, because when Peter G had a little peep into his cousin's soul, he found a fierce happiness and a snuggly feeling that was strange but somehow right. He managed to pass the rings over at the right moment. He took charge of Granny Clover's green joy ring, which had done its part, and slipped it safely into a pocket of his special shirt. When that was done, he reached up to put his hand on Peter P's shoulder when the handing over promise came. He had practised the words, but he wasn't entirely sure what they meant. It seemed that he, as Peter P's friend and support, was extending his friendship to include Pia at the same level and he was handing his best friend over into Pia's care.

He hoped he would be able to help her if he was ever needed.

Maybe when I have a wife, we can do this, too, and she and Mistress Pia will be part of —

The thought wasn't finished, then, because he didn't know enough to finish it.

Pia looked pretty, he thought, in a long green tunic with an embroidered overdress and a soft green shawl. The tunic belonged to her mother, Mistress Tess Tillien, and he heard Pia laugh and promise that if she ever had daughters, they, too, would be offered a chance to wear the family gown.

After the wedding, they had a party, with dancing, and Peter G danced with Mistress Alba, who was Pia's sister. She was fourteen, and she kissed him on the cheek.

"No harm," she murmured.

"No harm," he responded, laughing. He knew that was the correct response for when you didn't know someone very well, but you still kissed them or cuddled them in friendship. It showed them you wanted them to feel safe and comfortable with you. Dancing was fun, but he wished Gentie had been able to come. He thought she was a better size for holding onto when he danced.

He danced with other ladies, too, and then he went to Granny Clover and gave her back the green ring. He thought Peter should have done that, but Peter was kissing Pia, and he didn't want to disturb them.

Granny Clover kissed the ring and put it back on her finger. "Back again, old friend!" She hugged Peter G and said he'd been a fine steward. Then she tapped the ring and said, "Salix Peter, if you get wish matched one day, and mind, I'm not advising it since your grandad doesn't advise it, then come to me and ask for this ring for your miss to wear for a while. And when I've gone to glory —"

"No!" he burst out.

"I will, one day, but not for a good few years yet! But when I go to glory, I'm not taking this ring with me. I'll be so full of joy by then I'll have enough to fill me for eternity. So, when everyone's sad I've gone but happy for my joy, I lay it on you to see that this ring stays in the family. You can be its steward until you hand the job to someone else." She raised her brows at him. "All right, my Salix Peter?"

Not many people called him that.

He said, "All right, Granny."

CHAPTER ELEVEN: SOUP

The Pixie Forest. November 1950
Peter G

When the wedding was over, life went back to what Peter G thought of as ordinary with a shift. He went on visiting his friends at the cottage, but he was always careful to let them know when he was coming.

The first time he came, Pia scooped him up and kissed him hard on the brow, and he laughed and kissed her back. She was still hugging him when he realised her attention had shifted to Peter P, who was standing behind him. He glanced around and saw Peter P's turquoise eyes had widened just a little.

Gone pixie, Rory Inkersoll's voice said in his mind.

"Peter," Pia said.

Peter G whispered, "Put me down," and she did.

He went over to his cousin and hugged him, too. "No harm with Pia and me. Not ever," he said, and he felt Peter P relax and hug him back.

Gentie called him two weeks after that, and he jumped up happily and stepped into their private meeting place.

"Greet you, my lady Gentie!" He always called her that, because it made her giggle.

"Master Peter!" She ran to him, and they stood smiling at one another. He'd tried to explain to her that he was Peter G, but he was always Master Peter to her.

Gentie was a little shorter than him, and she had curly hair that bounced on her shoulders. It was a pretty shade of red-brown, like a bay pony, and she had soft sage green eyes. He could never tell what she wore, only that it was a dull green in colour and very plain. It came to her ankles, he thought, but he wasn't sure.

"Can you see my new clothes?" he asked.

"Tell me about them, and I might be able to."

"Long pants, not pixie britches, and a jerkin and shirt instead of a tunic. They're brown and green and the shirt's cream with a curly pattern embroidered in green. It's a big shirt to grow with. It's dashing."

She narrowed her eyes and stared at him for a time. "I see them! You look handsome. What have you been doing in your dashing shirt?"

He told her about the wedding, and his role in it, and how he would one day be the steward of his grandmother's wish match ring. After that, he told her his half-formed thought that in years to come he and his bride might be best true friends with Peter and Pia. "Does that sound silly?" he added.

"Nothing you say is silly, Master Peter. You know that." She grinned at him, eyes brimming over with fun. "I made barley soup today. It was good."

"Did you add parsley, so it's not that funny colour?"

"Of course. I brought some for you to try."

"I wish I could."

"I think you can. I think we can. Close your eyes."

"But then I can't see you."

"You might be able to feel me, though."

Peter G closed his eyes and held out his hands. He felt . . . nothing—not even the ground under his feet. He never did when he was with Gentie in their private meeting place.

It wasn't a very nice place, except that Gentie was there.

He was braving the disappointment when something

touched his bottom lip.

A wooden spoon. He shaped up to it and sipped, tasting soup.

Mmm. He wanted more, but when he opened his eyes, there was nothing but mist.

"My lady?"

"Here, Master Peter." He almost felt a brush of breath on his cheek. After a few seconds, he saw her again, paler than usual.

"Are you all right?"

"Of course, I am. I'm always all right when I'm with you. Did you taste my soup?"

He said eagerly, "It was fine. Did you put marigold petals in it?"

She clapped her hands. "I did! How clever of you to notice! Are you working well?"

"Grandad Grene is pleased with me."

"Good. I keep wishing I could be with you really, but it doesn't seem to work. I can't go because I don't know where you are."

He felt the same way. He knew where he was, but he'd never been able to tell her.

"Maybe when we go *over there*, we can find one another," she said.

"But that's a long time away."

"Three years. And then we go again when we're fifteen."

"We need to use the same gateway and go through hand-in-hand," he said.

"I know. Can you remember yours yet?"

"No. You?" he asked dolefully.

"No." He saw her stamp her foot with a burst of impatience. "I need to remember. So do you. How are we going to do this? I tried writing it down, but I can't see it."

He ventured, "Maybe if we put the words in a song it might

work. You know how when you sing you don't know the second verse words for sure until you come to them and there
they are? And when you sing, you don't have to remember
how to say a word."

"Yes! Yes! How clever of you!"

He tried to look modest.

"We have to go now," she said.

"No . . ."

"Yes! Hug yourself, Master Peter, and pretend it's my arms
around you. *No harm.*"

He wrapped his arms around himself and echoed, "*No
harm.* My lady? You do the same for me." He closed his eyes,
but he knew she'd already gone.

Gentie never stayed very long, and Peter G always felt sad
and lonely when she went. The feeling would persist for a
couple of days, but he knew he'd always go to her whenever
she called him. She was his lady Gentie.

Peter G chose *the Pixies' Wedding* as the song to set his gate
name to music. He knew it well, having practised it and sung
it with the other witnesses while Peter and Pia kneeled before
Grandad Grene for the blessing. It was a special song, and
Grandad Grene said it could be sung only when both parts of
a couple were pixies. Braefolk had their special song, and so
did tegs and courtfolk.

"What if they're like Master Rory?"

Rory Inkersoll was a scatterblood, which meant his ances-
tors included a lot of different orders.

"Then he chooses his own song to fit with his lady."

Peter G hoped he might wed a pixie miss when his time
came, so he could use the same song as Peter and Pia.

He worked out the new words and tried them out on Peter
P's goats. He didn't want to tell anyone else what he was doing because no one really understood about his friendship

with Gentie.

Down through the pixie forest to the pixie forest gate. Hands out, hands joined, and on to the olden copse.

It didn't rhyme, but the rhythm was right.

He sat down and took some gingerbread out of his pockets. He wasn't carrying much, so he had to break it into lots of tiny pieces for the goats to share. Snick, the biggest billy, snatched the first piece and then stood back, his beard jerking as he chewed, staring at Peter G with his funny yellow eyes.

"Come, Shilly — come, Lapis — come, Tarn . . ." He went through the whole flock and then, feeling self-conscious, he sang his lines over until they seemed more set than the original words.

"Come, Shilly — come, Lapis — come, Tarn — come, Ferry — come, Darlin . . ." He called them off and continued, "Down through the pixie forest to the pixie forest gate. Hands out, hands joined, and on to the olden copse."

When he thought he had it engraved in his memory, he hugged himself and then broke off, feeling uncomfortable.

"Gentie? Gentie?" She wasn't there.

The cottage door opened and Pia looked out. She saw Peter G among the goats and beckoned to him.

She wore a pixie tunic and pants. These were day wear, but her hair looked a little tumbled as if she'd been lying down. "Peter G! We're going swimming, remember? Why are you loitering out there with the goats?"

"I was singing." He ran to her and waved to Peter P as he erupted from the doorway and nearly knocked Pia off her feet. His hands shot out to steady her.

"Fuck it! Sorry. All right, my miss?"

She smiled up at him. "Of course."

"There's no fucking of course about it."

"Language, Peter."

He laughed and tucked his arms around her. "Pete, you ready?"

Peter G put the gateway song out of his mind. "Can you conjure me some gingerbread? I've run out."

Peter P flicked his fingers, and a big treacly slab appeared in his hand.

"Don't you get that on my tunic," Pia said.

Peter tossed it to Peter G. "Sooner you can conjure for yourself the better."

"Only five years or so to go," Peter G said gloomily. He didn't ask why life was so unfair as to make a person eleven years old before he or she could conjure. Grandfather Fen had explained it in his gentle way.

"See, Pete, some little folk might conjure something when they shouldn't."

"But conjuring can't be used for harm."

"No-o, but think if a little babby felt a bit hungry, and his mum was busy stirring pudding. That babby might try to conjure milk and get cold milk from the larder instead of his mum's loving supply."

"I'm not a baby."

"I know. I doubt you'd ever try to conjure the wrong thing, but it is what it is. Some things that are good things, and even wonderful things, aren't right until the time is right. You be patient, and good things will come. And Pete?"

"Mm?"

"Can you let your mum and dad look after you a bit? You're the only Peter they have."

"I'll try."

He tried.

CHAPTER TWELVE: BARBARA ALLEN

Windhill. Boxing Day, 1950
Barbie Hanover

Barbie felt wrong in her skin. She was afraid, resolute, and curiously numb. She gazed at herself in the long looking glass of the room she'd had since she was five.

She was too old to be back there, but she didn't know where else to be.

"Barbie, Jacobi's here," her mother called.

"Coming."

Her mother had known Jacobi for years, so she had no qualms about inviting him in to wait for Barbie to be ready.

"Barbie!"

If that was Peter, he'd come bounding up the stairs with those weird eyes glowing. He wouldn't sit on a settee and wait for me.

Bother. Peter had ambushed her again.

I'll never get rid of him now.

She pulled on a loose cardigan and flicked up her hair. Then she studied the small flat parcel on her dressing table. Yes or no?

No.

Give it to him.

Barbie, you can't do this to Jacobi. Not possibly. He's a good man. He loves you.

Yes, and that's why you can't do this to him.

"Coming."

Her mum had been cooking poached eggs. *Something light*

after all that Christmas Dinner.

Barbie wished she wouldn't. The way that yellow yolk oozed out of the not-quite-set white made her feel peculiar. At the same time, she wanted to paint it. Maybe she would. She'd set up the corner of her room as a studio.

She walked sedately to the living room, where Jacobi got up to greet her. He looked somehow drained, and her heart jolted with anxiety.

"Are you all right?"

"I am now." He offered her a small parcel. "Merry Christmas, my Barbara Allen."

He still called her that, after the song. She'd never minded but then, two weeks ago when she'd been feeling sad and scared, she'd asked Meredith Oak about it. Meredith had trained as a music teacher, and she obligingly looked out her books of folk songs. One seemed to be in a foreign language, although Meredith said it was really an old form of English.

"*Me Lovien Woldë*. It means *to love me well*," she said. The song they wanted wasn't in that, but it turned up in another book called *Merrily We*. "There's a catch in this one. I mean, a round. *Merrily we dance the round,* it starts. And here's *Barbara Allen,* which isn't so merry."

Barbie reached for the book, but Meredith hung on. "Sorry, Barb, but this one's a present from my lad. It's charmed, and I'm not sure what effect it might have on a human." She pulled a little face and continued, "There are lots of versions of the song, but they're generally about a man called William who dies because a girl, Barbara Allen, doesn't love him. She won't come to comfort him when he's dying, but afterwards, she feels bad about that, and she dies, too, of remorse."

"That really cheers me up," Barbie said.

"Oh, but they're buried side by side, and a rose comes from his heart and a brier from hers, and they grow wrapped together." Meredith grimaced. "I think it's meant to be romantic, but it's creepy, really."

It was. Barbie remembered the rose Jacobi gave her when she was fifteen.

Meredith patted her curls. "Like my new 'do?"

"It's pretty." Barbie squinted at Meredith's ears. They *were* a bit pointed.

Jacobi was still holding out the parcel.

"Thank you." Barbie hesitated, a little uneasy. "I have something for you, too. I left it in my room."

Her mum said indulgently, "Barbie! You'd forget your head if it wasn't screwed on."

Barbara took the gift and hurried to get Jacobi's. She hoped he liked it. Maybe she should have bought him something instead, but this had seemed right. She'd decided not to give it to him because it was too personal, but now he'd given her something, it would be appropriate.

She came back with both parcels, and they opened them together.

He'd got her earrings in the shape of red roses, embellished with ruby hearts. "Oh, Jacobi!" Tears started in her eyes.

Her mother looked as pleased as punch. "I think those merit a kiss, my girl."

She pecked him on the cheek.

Lemonade.

Her uneasy tummy settled.

Jacobi opened his present.

"I hope you like it," she said.

She'd painted a miniature portrait of him and Johnny, back when they were seventeen, sitting on the settee. Johnny had a smudge on his cheek and grey knees. Jacobi was neat and clean, as he always had been.

Barbie clenched her hand around the dainty earrings. Would he see it? She'd deliberately half-screened it in a fold of his shirt.

Yes.

His finger traced the figures and lingered on the curve of the red rose.

"Barbie, you could at least have painted Johnny looking less of a ragamuffin," her mother chided.

"But he did. He still does."

Johnny, asking Peter for some of his blood, smudged with ink and with a coffee stain on his white coat . . .

"That's him to a tee, Missus Hanover," Jacobi said. "What a pair we were then."

"It's been a long while," Barbie said.

"I'll treasure this. A Barbara Hanover original!"

"Could be worth a fortune," she said straight-faced. She knew she was good. She also knew she wasn't good enough to make much of an impression as a portrait painter. She'd recently picked up a job illustrating a storybook for children. She had to earn some money, and she needed a way to do it without having to go to an office to type.

She had decided to model two of the characters in the story on the young Johnny and Jacobi, which in turn had given her the idea of painting the portrait.

Jacobi tucked the little frame in his pocket and got to his feet. "We'll be off, then. Bye, Missus Hanover."

Barbie said, "Just a mo." She went back to her room, removed her pink Lucite earrings and replaced them with the roses. They looked lovely, glowing with promise. She was uneasily aware that after today, she might never wear them again.

They went to the beach and walked along the sand. Barbie kicked her shoes off, and Jacobi took them from her without hesitation.

"I want to paddle."

He said, "Give me your bag, then."

She gave him her handbag. It was a new one her mother and father had given her for Christmas. How many boys would hold a girl's handbag and shoes while she paddled?

The cold waves curled around her toes. She splashed around and then came back up on the beach. "Ugh, sand."

"I can fix that for you."

"Can you really?"

He glanced about. There was no one very near. "Lift your foot."

She did so, swayed and grabbed for his arm.

"Steady, Barbara Allen." He flicked his fingers, and the damp sand dried abruptly and fell off her foot. He did the other.

"Elf magic?"

"We don't do magic."

He smiled at her, but she saw his eyes were strained.

"What's the matter, Jacobi?"

"I have something to tell you."

"Oh? Should we sit down?"

"No. Better do this standing up. And Barbie, if this upsets you, please just stay calm and tell me you want to go home. I'll take you there right away. Please, please don't upset your-self."

This sounded bad. Barbie's heart thudded with dread.

"Don't look like that."

"Just tell me."

His cheeks went dull pink. "You know what I am."

"Well, yes. You told me years ago, and you just reminded me by conjuring the sand off for me."

"You also know our family has lived *over here* for a very long time. We live like humans. We are almost exactly like humans, except for a couple of things."

"Conjuring and the pointy ears," she said, trying to lighten the atmosphere.

"There's one other thing. We don't usually talk about this to anyone outside the fay community, because it's embarrass-ing. It's . . . some people would find it shocking. Even I do when I'm in my right mind."

Barbie's heart was still thudding, and she started to feel sick.

That thing Peter did . . . ugh.

Jacobi went on, "You know how some people drink too much or smoke too much. Mostly they know they shouldn't. They probably decide not to do it ever again, but then they do it anyway because they can't help themselves."

She remembered having three sherries. Peter had stopped her from having more.

But I don't often do that — only a couple of times.

"And some people drive too fast or gamble. They know it's bad for them, but they can't help it."

"Jacobi, please stop. I know about addiction. Johnny told me. Do you get drunk? Or gamble?" She couldn't imagine it.

"No! I don't get drunk. Actually, I can't. Alcohol doesn't have any effect on me."

"What's this about then?"

He went even pinker. "Around Christmas. You've noticed I don't go to church on Christmas Eve?"

"You mean elves aren't Christians?"

"Yes. Well, some of us are. But around Christmas, we start to feel restless. We need something special from someone to make it go away."

His discomfort made his meaning plain.

"You need to lie down with someone and . . . make love."

"Sort of. Only it's not about love. It can be, for those of us who have a wife. If we don't, we have to find someone else."

"You need a girlfriend to do it?"

He looked even more miserable. "Or else we go to a special place down in the city where other elves go, too. It's a secret bar in the back of the *Pear Tree* pub. We find someone who needs it, too, and then we help one another."

"Are you asking me to make love with you, so you don't need to go there?"

"No! The time's passed. It was on Christmas Eve."

"Then you're saying you went to this place. And you made love with some elf woman. My God, was it Meredith? Or Sylvie?"

"Meredith has a boyfriend. I expect she went to him."

"Sylvie, then."

Ugh.

She swallowed, feeling revulsion.

"Barbie, please! I didn't want to. I don't want to. Every year I promise myself I'll be stronger next year."

"*Every* year?"

"Since I was eighteen. That's when the thing started. It's natural, to elves. In the old days, people got married earlier, so it wasn't a problem."

She tried to push down her nausea. "Why did you tell me this?"

"Because I'm in love with you. I would dearly like to have you as my wife. I'd *never* need to go to the release bar if I had you unless you couldn't bear the idea of me needing that sort of attention. It's not just once, you see. It can be two or three times or more in the night." He sounded utterly miserable.

Barbie opened her mouth to speak and then abruptly clapped her hand over her lips and bolted for the bushes that rimmed the dry sand.

She retched and threw up.

Jacobi came and put a gentle hand on her shoulder. "I'm so sorry." He sounded about to cry.

Barbie groped for a handkerchief, kicking sand over the icky pool. She heard him snap his fingers, and then he handed her a warm washcloth.

Gratefully, she wiped her face.

He gave her a little bottle of lemonade with the cork already pulled.

Barbie drank some and burst into tears.

"I'm so sorry. I'll understand if you can't bear to look at

me," he said in a shadow of his usual voice.

She mopped at her face, and he handed her a large, dry handkerchief.

She chuckled weakly. "Oh, Jacobi, you're a card. You're like a magician pulling rabbits out of a hat."

"Does this mean there's a chance for me?"

She felt more affection for him than she ever had.

I could make him happy, and everything will be all right.

Barbie, you can't. *He'd never forgive you.*

She drank more of the lemonade to give herself courage.

"I have something to confess to you. You might never be able to look at *me* again. Can we sit down? I don't feel so good."

He guided her away to a shady area and conjured a large beach towel for them to sit on. He put his arm lightly around her shoulders. "Nothing you could do would make me love you less."

"Are you sure?"

"Elf's honour."

"Is that like the boy scout thing?"

"No, I just made it up."

His attempt to lighten the situation fell flat.

"Mine's worse than yours. Much worse, because it can't be kept secret and it's not just for a few days."

He reached down and touched her stomach. He'd never done such a thing before. "Hello, in there," he said gently.

More tears flooded from Barbie's eyes. "You knew."

"I thought, maybe. You look a little bit different, and you're pale."

"How can you possibly want to marry me?"

"You're still the girl I've loved for years."

"I don't want to have it adopted. I know that's what people mostly do, but I'd hate it to grow up feeling as if I didn't want it. I mean, I didn't want it. Don't. But it's done now, and I expect I'll love it. Johnny says most people do."

"You told Johnny?"

"No! It was just one of those things he said once."

"I wouldn't ask you to give it up. I just have a couple of questions, but there's no blame to you, not now, not ever. If you marry me, this will be our baby — yours and mine."

She sobbed for a while, and then he said, "You met this chap in Appledore?"

She choked a yes.

"Do you still love him?"

That was more difficult. She thought of Peter and managed a wry smile. "I never did. I was fond of him. He was sweet and funny, sometimes. Young."

"Then why did —" He broke off.

Barbie said, "He was a pixie man called Peter. We dated a bit, and I taught him to drive in Johnny's car. He was —" She thought better of telling Jacobi about the modelling. She had done it, too, but although her conscience was perfectly clear, she thought Jacobi mightn't understand. She continued, "He made friends with an old artist . . . a has-been, who was making one last try at some kind of big canvas. The old man was a drunk, and he died in hospital. Johnny was there, and he let Peter stay until the old man went. Then Peter came back to the hostel. I went to see him, and he was so sad. He said he felt cold."

She found it impossible to describe the state Peter had been in, but Jacobi clearly understood. "It's called soul-cold. Horrible. So, of course, you took pity on the poor chap."

"Not right away. He asked, and I said no, but well, it happened in the end. We had rubbers a friend gave me, but one of them broke."

"A pixie man shouldn't have needed rubbers."

"You mean, that's true? He said that, but I thought he was trying it on."

"It's true. But I suppose if he thought the rubber was

working, he wouldn't have felt the need to hold hard." He laughed bitterly. "Oh, my Barbara Allen, what a mess. Does he know?"

She said, "No! I didn't know myself until long after I came home. And I didn't tell him when it broke. I thought it would be all right. It wasn't until I – um – " She put her hands over her cheeks.

"I thought that was why you came home."

"No. I didn't know at that stage. I just knew I couldn't be with him. Couldn't sleep with him. It wasn't his fault. I just couldn't – "

"You don't love him, then?"

"Not like that. No." She shuddered and scrubbed her face with her hands.

"Barbie, look at me."

She shook her head.

Jacobi put his finger under her chin and turned her to face him, so her hands slipped down. "Barbie, I love you. I want us to be happy together. You and me, and the little one, and maybe some other babies, later."

"But what will people say?"

He let her go. "They'll say plenty, but let them think we were so in love we couldn't wait. It could have been true. This is *our* baby. I'll love him or her because I love you."

"What about your parents? They'll guess, because they know when I came home. You hadn't visited me in Appledore since that time."

Since that time, you found out Johnny had moved, and you asked me to come home.

He laughed. "Mum loves babies. All elves do. Lots of us are midwives, or nursery nurses, or kindergarten teachers. You'll see, Mum and Dad will be over the moon to see me happy at last. They *know* how hard I've been finding it. They knew how it knocked me when you went south. I've hated having to go to the release bar, although the other elves there are mostly in the same situation."

"Why did it bother you, then, if there are others, and if it's natural to you?"

"Because I only ever wanted to be with you. And it wasn't fair to the other girls to be with them when I was thinking of you, and I couldn't bear to think of you when I was . . . oh, I'm making a mess of this."

She turned to him.

Others. He's been with more than one girl. At least with me, it was only Peter, and only because he was so unhappy. The first time, anyway.

"If you really want me, I'd love to marry you, but I have a couple of things to clear up before I say *yes*."

"Go on."

"I'll never ask you about the girls you slept with. It's not my business, and you did nothing wrong. You helped them, and they helped you. In return, I hope you'll never throw it back at me about *this* . . ." She patted her still-flat stomach. "And you'll never say *I told you so* and remind me I should have come home when you asked me to."

"Never, my Barbara Allen. I promise."

"And I'd rather you didn't call me *Barbara Allen* anymore. Meredith told me about the song. The woman in it was so stupid. She let a man die and then she died, too. I might have been stupid sometimes, but I'm not ever going to be that stupid again."

Jacobi stared at her. "I had no idea about the song. I just thought it was a love ballad, like *Annie Laurie*."

"It's not. It's about two people who ruined their lives. We *won't* do that."

"You'll marry me then?" The light in his eyes almost made her start crying again.

She said in a rush, "Before I say *yes*, I need you to make love to me and stay with me all night. Will you do that?"

"You don't want to wait?"

"No. I have to *know*. If it's the way it was with Peter, I can't say yes, because you'll be needing . . . it . . . and I won't be able to do it. And I *won't* turn into Barbara Allen."

He put his arms around her. "Barbie, Barbie, what am I going to do with you?"

"Kiss me, maybe?"

He kissed her, gently, and then he put his hand on her tummy again and said, "Little one, your mum's just made your dad the happiest man in the world."

Chapter Thirteen: Hard Work

The Cottage, Pixie Forest. December 1951
Pia Peckerdale

Marriage to Peter was a glorious affair for Pia. It was fun, deeply fulfilling, crammed with love and laughter and lit by occasional sparks when Peter got a notion into his head which had to be got out. Occasionally it was she who had the notion, and she tried to be fair about that.

Melody's arrival a few weeks before midsummer in the year after her parents' wedding was one such time.

Pia's labour was fast and hard, and she wanted Peter to be in two places at once. Her back hurt, and she wanted him to hold her and kiss her through the pain, but she also wanted him to receive their baby into his hands.

When Peter protested that he couldn't do both at the same time, and they needed to call someone else, she stormed at him that he could do it, because he had to and it was all his fault anyway.

That riled Peter because, as he put it, he might have forgotten to hold back one blissful day or night when his willy was held so snugly in Pia's nether pixie grip, but she'd undoubtedly also forgotten to close the little doorway that, left carelessly open, had welcomed his swimmers and let one snuggle up in comfort to build their baby.

"Language, Peter!" Pia yelled when he'd finished giving his protestation.

"Why the fuck are you bothered about that now?" he

104

yelled back.

Pia screamed with pain and frustration.

Peter grabbed her and kissed her fiercely. "Sorry, sorry, oh fuck, I wish there was something I could do to help you."

"There is," she mumbled against his mouth. "Hold me and receive our baby."

"I can't do both!"

"Dad did it for Mum."

"Your dad's a fucking fix-it pixie. I'm just a pixie."

"You're not just a pixie. You're my Peter."

"Right." Peter let her go, and she wailed in protest as another pain gathered her into its grip.

He conjured pillows into a heap and braced himself against them, legs apart. When the contraction eased, he lifted Pia to sit with her legs hooked over his and her back against his chest. "Remember this?"

"Yes. You bent down and kissed my thigh and played with me before you gave me the first friendly." She gritted her teeth as another pain hit her.

"All right. We're going to get this done properly." His arms came around her, and he bent around to kiss her cheek.

Sobbing, she turned her mouth to his, and they kissed in a welter of salt tears.

The pain still gripped her, but it seemed far away. This was her Peter, her love, and he was going to make this work.

He bent forward, reaching down, and Pia felt an overwhelming desire to push. She caught her breath and pushed with all her might.

"I've got her! Can you push again?"

Pia panted, and the feeling built, so she pushed again, pressing her legs out against Peter's taut muscles.

"Got her."

Pia's head spun, and she felt Peter conjure most of the pillows away, so they lay down. He rolled her off, so they were facing one another, with the baby between them.

"You've got to kiss her," she said.

He leaned in and kissed the baby, holding it in his big hands, and then spluttered and conjured a cloth to wipe the tiny face clean.

"Never mind that. Wrap her up." Pia felt strangely calm now the pain had gone.

Peter conjured a shawl and wrapped the baby, leaving her little arms free.

Pia noted it was her wedding shawl, the softest thing she'd ever owned.

Never mind. It will wash.

She gestured to him to tuck the baby down between them.

"You're all fucking sticky," Peter observed.

"So are we all. You'll have to cut the cord."

He looked worried.

"It won't hurt us."

She hoped to be able to rest a bit, but there was more to do, and she needed cleaning up along with their baby, and then the baby wailed, and she had to feed it. Her.

The baby had black hair like Peter's, and she smelled of clove carnations. She was the most beautiful baby ever born.

They named her Melody Sunshine, and she was a joy and a delight from the beginning.

Chapter Fourteen: The White Place

The White Place. 1952
Peter G

The plan to sing his gateway address to Gentie didn't work for Peter G. He put off trying for months because he wanted to hold on to hope, but finally, when early summer warmed the forest again, he made the attempt.

If he had been the screaming type, he might have yelled with frustration when he opened his mouth to sing the address to his lady Gentie and found he was singing off the names of Peter P's goats instead.

"Come, Shilly — come, Lapis — come, Tarn — come, Ferry — come, Darlin . . ." He broke off with a shake of his head. "No. Come, Shilly — come, Lapis — come, Tarn — come, Ferry — come, Darlin . . . Hurry — Flanna — and Bertold — and Shug . . ."

He stopped, heart thudding with disappointment. "Sorry, my lady. You try."

She smiled at him. She'd had a gap in her teeth, but now her big front teeth were in, and her smile was a different shape.

"Pumpkin and barley with marigold . . ."

She stopped.

"Now you're making fun of me," Peter G said, clinging to hope.

"No." She tried again. "Three-cornered leeks and ginger — Oh!" She shook her head.

107

"Is that a soup recipe?"

"Yes. But I never made a song about that. I made one for the gateway address and another one for where I live."

"Isn't that the alplands?"

"No. I don't think so. Maybe. Why do you think that?"

"You told me about the bogles."

Her face cleared. "My sister-by-love comes from the alplands. It's a long way from where I live. I think."

"Try the place you live," Peter G urged.

Gentie tried, but what came from that song was a list of herbs.

"What's your last name, my lady?"

"I'm Gentian—Oh!" She stamped her foot soundlessly.

"I'm Peter G."

"Gee?"

"The letter G. That's because my big cousin is Peter P."

"So, it could be Peter Gareth or Peter Glen, or Peter Gervais? The way I'm Gentian Geileis?"

"No, it's part of my last name. My real first name is Salix, so I'm Salix Peter, but I'm always called Peter G."

She said, "It's something."

"Not enough."

"Not enough," she echoed. She sighed and said, "We have to go now."

"No! Please stay. We can try again."

"I can't, Master Peter. Someone's calling me."

He felt a flash of hot jealousy and blinked in astonishment. *No. Mine.*

He turned wide eyes on his friend, who belonged to someone else who had the right to call her away. "Please stay for me."

"I have to go. Hug yourself and pretend it's my arms around you."

She was gone. He didn't hug himself. He stood in the mist until things went blurry, and then there was nothing much until he woke up.

"Pete? Darling?" His mother's anxious face looked down at him.

"Mm?" He stretched.

Russet put her arms around him. "What's the matter, Pete? You've slept half the day away."

"I feel cold." He shivered.

"You stay in bed, and I'll bring you some soup."

He cried then.

His mother sat with him, and then his father came and asked if he should conjure a note to tell Grandad Grene he couldn't come for lessons.

Peter G tried to warm himself on thoughts of the patterns in numbers, but the white place got in the way.

"Is there anyone you want to see?" His mother looked down at him again.

"Gentie."

"Oh, Pete, I'd help you if I could, but I don't know how. Will I try reading you?"

Russet read folk with ease, far better than Peter G could, but he didn't want her looking into his soul. Not since that flash of unreasoning anger that someone else could take his friend away. He didn't recognise himself in an angry Peter G.

He shook his head.

"Do you want big Peter to come? Or Pia? She'd bring Melody for you to cuddle."

"No."

"Is there anyone you want?"

"Gentie."

"Anyone else?"

Peter G tried to focus his aching mind. A face swam into view. It was a broad face with big amber eyes and a triangular nose. "Can the red cat come?"

Russet glanced at Quercus and raised her eyebrows. He

must have nodded, because she said, "Dad will see if he can come."

Peter G folded up into himself, and, for the first time ever, he took himself to the white place where he met Gentie. Until that day he'd only ever seen her when she called him. He stood in the white mist, feeling its damp breath on his cheeks.

"Gentie? My lady?"

His voice was so muffled he wasn't sure anyone would hear it. He went on calling, but the mist threw his voice back to him.

Something touched his ankle, and he looked down, startled. The only thing he'd ever touched in that place was Gentie's wooden spoon. The thing that touched him was warm and alive.

He dropped to his knees before the red cat.

"Lawks a mercy."

The red cat wound around his legs, tail trailing after it. Peter G gathered it into his arms and held it. The cat rumbled a slow purr.

He moved from his knees to sitting with his legs outstretched and set the cat beside him. The warm tang of incense filled the air.

After a bit, he felt an arm close around his shoulders in a brief hug.

"Greet you, Master Rory," he said.

"And you, Master . . ." The young man looked down into his face. "Peter G."

"Yes. Can you tell me the rest of my name?"

"Grene. I think it's Salix Peter Grene, making you a pliable tree, a steadfast rock and the colour of growth and life. It's a fine, fine name for a pixie man."

"Thank you."

They sat together for a bit, and then Rory Inkersoll said, "Can you tell me where we are, Peter G?"

He turned up his hands. "It's the white place."

"Can you tell me why I'm here with you, then?"

"No. I asked for the red cat to come, and Mum said Dad would ask for him."

"That explains it, I suppose. The red cat can go places I can't and be where I'm not able to be. If you're here, I suppose he followed you. He can go through walls, you know."

"I saw him do that when Mistress Hillyard made my suit for the wedding. She saw him, too. She said *Lawks a mercy*. You're here now, though. So you must be able to come here the same as I can."

"Not *here*, Peter G. Your white place is probably limbo, so I can manage this quite easily. In a way, I've been in my own white place for days."

"By yourself?"

"Yes."

"Why? It's no fun alone."

"I can't be with my lassie because I can't accept the unacceptable."

Peter G looked up at him. "You don't have enough years to have a lassie — do you?"

"I have enough years for this." Rory removed his arm from Peter G's shoulders and showed him his long hand, bearing a copper ring with two bright yellow stones. "It's a kissing ring and a promise of more, but I don't know that I can wear it anymore. Not honestly."

"Why not? You can't kiss someone dishonestly . . . can you?"

The young man was silent, and Peter G thought he was probably wrestling with what to tell him. He had an inspiration. "*No harm* if you tell me. I *know* there are things you do with your miss . . . or your lassie . . . that are private. Just tell me the ordinary bits that are around them," he offered.

"Hm." Rory sounded distracted.

"Why does it have to make us unhappy?" Peter G heard the sob in his voice and swallowed.

"Loving someone? Well, it doesn't. It's a great gift. Loving friendship keeps the world joyful. What makes us unhappy is wanting what we can't and shouldn't have. The gift is to love what you can have and to accept what you can't have with grace."

"Can you do that?"

"I'm not doing that. That's why I might lose everything. What's your trouble, Peter G? Why did you need the red cat for company?"

"I have a friend called Gentie. She's my age, and I love being with her, but this is the only place I ever see her."

"Do you mean you don't know where she lives?"

"That's it. I can't find her, and she can't find me. When we're here, we don't know our last names or where we live."

"So that's why you asked me for your name."

"Yes. It's Salix Peter Grene. And I live—"

"You live in the pixie forest, not far from the manse, with Master Quercus and Mistress Russet Grene."

"Yes, I know that now. But when she's here, I don't remember."

"Do you have *the sight*?"

"*She* has that. She told me."

"There, then!" Rory sounded cheerful. "My lassie has *the sight*. It told her long ago that she'd meet the red cat, and then, eight years later, she'd meet a man, and she'd love him for all her life."

"Has she met him yet?"

"It's not eight years. There are seven days to go."

"Are you going to be him?"

"Yes. And she'll love me all her life, and then she'll leave me alone and go to glory. She's a lot older than me, you see."

"You'll have a lot of years to be loved before that happens."

"I have to find a way to make it enough for me. If I can't, then I won't get anything."

Peter G said reproachfully, "At least you'll get to be with her in proper life. You won't have to hug yourself and pretend it's her."

"You're right, of course. Is that what you do? Hug yourself and pretend?"

"Sometimes, but I don't want hugging. I just want to go swimming with her, and make soup, and show her how to make lavender cheese. Maybe we could play music or go dancing at the midsummer ball, just for fun. *No harm.*"

"You want to be true friends and do what true friends do. I think you and your—"

"Gentie. Gentian Geileis, she said, but we don't have the last name," Peter G supplied.

"Then you and your Gentie might have been borrowing ahead, by meeting in your white place before you can really know one another. When you meet properly, you'll be able to do all those things."

Put that way, it sounded almost comforting.

"When do you think we'll meet outside?"

"I can't say. It might be tomorrow, or a long time off, but waiting isn't so bad. Not when you know something beautiful is coming."

"I hope I can tell her that when she calls me again."

Rory gave him a friendly pat on the shoulder. "Why not?"

"I mightn't remember."

"I think you will, because you heard it *here.* You mightn't remember when you wake up at home, but you'll know when it counts. How do you get out of here? This probably isn't a place where you should come often, or stay too long."

"It's not too nice. Usually, Gentie says we have to go, and after a bit, I'm home."

"Would you like the red cat to wait with you until you go

home?"

Peter G turned to say *please,* but then he saw Rory's face, hollow and pale, with huge dark smudges under his eyes. "You've been crying."

"Only inside. Only when I'm here."

"You should go and be with your lassie while you can." He reached up and patted Rory's shoulder, offering comfort in turn. "I feel better now. I'd like to wait here in case Gentie comes. I don't think she'll come while you're here because she doesn't know you."

"All right. I'll go, but if you need someone to talk to, you can come and see me at the manse. I'm not a priest yet, but I'm a good listener."

"Are you going to see your lassie when you leave here?"

"Yes. Your Gentie has been borrowing friendship ahead, but I've been borrowing sorrow. I won't do it anymore."

They sat on together for a while, and then Rory folded into the red cat. It wound around Peter G, chirruped a farewell and swanned off into the mist.

Peter G stayed where he was until someone called his name.

"Master Peter?"

He got to his feet. "Here! Greet you, my lady Gentian."

She ran to him, stopping just out of reach. "You came quickly this time."

"I was already here."

She tilted her head. "You came by yourself? You never have before."

"I have now. Who called you away from me, last time? Do you have other friends like me?"

"No, you're my best friend, and you're the only one I see here. My mother called me. My sister-by-love is making me a dress, and I had to go to look at the cloth. Do you like it?" She twirled.

Peter G perceived she was wearing something new. He had trouble making it out, but it looked to be cream with green curly embroidery.

"It's very pretty," he said. He knew Pia liked it when Peter P said she looked fucking gorgeous. He also knew he wasn't meant to talk like Peter P.

Speaking Peter was a little secret he had with Pia. Pia said when Peter P said *fucking gorgeous,* he meant *very pretty,* and when Peter P said, *green-willied fucker,* he meant *another pixie man, or maybe a leprechaun gossoon.* An *old git* was an older person.

"It will be pretty," Gentie said.

"Isn't it pretty already?" He reached out as if he could touch the material. He thought it might feel soft like the shirt he'd had for Peter P's wedding. That still fitted him, although the pants were too small. He remembered Mistress Hillyard had said he'd be able to wear the shirt for a long time because the deep cuffs could fold down when he was taller. He was glad about that. It was his favourite shirt.

Gentie stopped twirling and put her hands on her hips. The cream tunic darkened into the sage green dress she always wore, which matched her eyes. "It's not made yet, Master Peter. I was showing you the way it's going to be. Currie says it's going to be special, with tucks, so I can wear it for a long time, even when I start to go woman-shape."

"Currie?"

"My sister-by-love." She leaned forward and peered at him. "You've been crying."

"Only a bit. It was because you wouldn't stay."

"I know. It makes me sad, too, when I go away from you. That's why I don't come here too often. Master Peter, can I tell you something I'm scared of?"

"Bogles?"

She giggled. "Not while I have gingerbread in my pocket.

Currie says if I ever see a bogle, it's probably someone with a bogle manifest, and gingerbread is bound to help."

"It works on goats," Peter G remarked. He leaned closer, catching the scent of green and growing things. He'd smelled that before in the white place. It wasn't the red cat's incense smell, or his own scent, which was sweet and peppery. It was Gentie. "What are you scared of, if it's not bogles? Maybe I can help."

"I don't think so. It's about *the sight.*"

He felt his heartbeat tripping fast. "My friend said *the sight* was letting you borrow ahead."

"What friend? Peter P?"

"No. This is another friend. His name's Rory. He's sometimes a red — "

"I think of it as *borrowing time,*" she burst out.

"Same thing."

"And that's what I'm afraid of! I'm afraid the time we spend together *now* is borrowed, and we'll have to pay it back one day."

"How do you pay back time?"

"I think the time we have used is time we'll miss when we can meet properly. If we use all our time *here,* there might be none left for *there.*"

Peter G thought of Rory's dread of years spent without the lassie he loved. He knew the lassie was older than Rory, and that meant she'd die before him. He supposed Peter P and Pia would die before he did. They were twenty now. He was eight. His parents and his grandparents and everyone he loved were older still. Only little Melody was younger, and she'd be left alone one day. The thought made him feel cold.

She needs someone. I'll wish for her to be loved forever.

He looked steadily at Gentie, gazing at her lovely warm curly hair and her green eyes.

"You're a pixie miss . . . aren't you?"

"Yes, of course."

"My lady . . . No, Gentie. You're not a lady yet."

She pouted at him.

"I should think you're about eight, like me. A little miss."

"Nearly nine. Not a *little* miss. A medium miss. But how did you know?"

He tapped his new front teeth. "You have these, too. Peter P says I look like a fucking rabbit, but that my face will grow into them."

Gentie said, "You don't look like a rabbit. I never see you very well, but I expect you're handsome."

"I'm not, really. I'm eight, and I have rabbit teeth. Mum says I have nice eyes, and the rest of me will catch up. Listen, Gentie. What if you're right, and we have to pay back time?"

She shrugged.

"Do you think we should stop borrowing time and wait to be friends when we really meet, and when we can do stuff like swimming and dancing instead of just talking?"

He wanted her to say *no*.

She said, "I don't want to not see you, but waiting might be safer."

He quoted, "Waiting isn't so bad when you know something beautiful is coming."

"Not so bad," she said. She touched her chin. "Am I beautiful, do you think?"

"I don't know. I love—I mean, I like the way you look, but I can't tell if it's real or what I imagine."

"I have knobbly knees. The bones are growing fast."

"I don't see that."

"That's because I have a tunic on."

He didn't really want to talk about the way they looked or what they wore. He thought he'd spent most of his life talking to people because they did things he couldn't do. He liked it when Peter and Pia went swimming with him, or when they took Melody on a picnic. That was more fun than just talking at the cottage. "Let's make this goodbye for now," he said.

"You won't forget me?"

"Never! Gentian Geileis, I'll never forget you."

"And I won't forget you, Peter G."

"We have to go." It was the first time he'd ever said it to her.

"Yes. Until we meet for the first time," she said. "Hug yourself and —"

"No! I won't be doing that. Borrowing hugs might mean doing without, later. I'm going to wait until you can hug me properly."

She turned and walked away, farther into the white place.

Peter G called after her, "Gentie, remember — my name is Peter Grene! Salix Peter Grene, for a pliant tree, a steadfast rock and the colour of growing things."

He had no idea if she heard him.

He stood in the mist, watching it fade around him, and then he blinked. He was lying in his bed on an early summer afternoon.

His mother was holding his hand. "Do you feel better?" she asked.

He nodded against the pillow. He didn't feel better. He felt empty.

"The red cat came for a while. He sat with you and purred, but then he went off. I don't think —" Her voice broke off.

"Master Rory has been borrowing sorrow," Peter G said.

"I believe he has, the poor lad. You did see him then?"

"I don't know. I think so." He sat up.

"Where are you off to?"

"I'm going to the manse. Grandad Grene has some new number puzzles for me. I want to think about that."

Russet conjured him some bread and cheese from the larder, and he ate it on his way to the manse.

When he arrived, his grandfather was busy in the study.

"Peter G! Your dad said you wouldn't be coming today, so I've arranged to go to the castle."

"I slept too long. Is Master Rory here?"

"No, he went to visit Mistress Drumwiddy."

"You know lots of people at the castle," Peter G said.

Grandad Grene put down his pen and looked at him thoughtfully. "What's wrong, Peter G?"

"I thought you might know some lads my age there."

"I do indeed. I teach some of them."

"Could I go there sometime?"

"You can come today, if you like. I thought you enjoyed having lessons alone."

He said, "I'm going *over there* next year for my first visit. It will be scary. I'd like to know other lads who are going, too. They don't have to be pixies."

Grandad Green said, "That is a fine idea. Shall we go now? Joe Bakewell is visiting there at present. His grandfather is my cousin. His mum's a halfling and his dad's human. Joe's just a couple of years older than you, so he's a good person to tell you a bit about living *over there*."

"If he lives *over there*, and he's mostly human, why is he here?"

"He's come to learn our ways, so you can help him, too."

CHAPTER FIFTEEN: MIXED FEELINGS

The Cottage, Pixie Forest. 1952
Peter Peckerdale

Melody was running around, talking a little, playing with the goats and enchanting everyone she met. Her dark hair gleamed like a crow's wing, and she bubbled over with interest and fun.

Occasionally she got cross and screamed until the cottage rang with her wails, but it never lasted long.

Peter loved his daughter deeply, but he occasionally regretted that day, or night, when he'd forgotten to hold. He couldn't say that to Pia, because she'd yell at him, and he'd deserve it. Neither could he say anything to Peter G, who had been having some kind of wobble of his own. There was no one he could talk to about his occasional regret, and he was ashamed of himself for having it.

One day, he saw Pia wearing a new tunic and reached for her. "That's fucking gorgeous, my miss!"

"Language, Peter. Remember Melody."

As if I could forget.

He scooped up his daughter as she whirled past and blew a blast of air against her tummy. Melody squealed with laughter.

"Dad-Dad."

"My little miss. My *gorgeous* little miss." He hugged her, and she burrowed under his chin.

Peter was disconcerted. Pia did that when she wanted

loving.

He caught Pia's gaze and relaxed. "How did we make this between us?"

"I believe you forgot to hold," Pia said tartly.

"If you knew how it feels when you use that pixie grip on him down there . . ." His willy twitched at the memory, and he was glad he was wearing loose britches.

"I know. I forgot to close up . . . You make me feel so loved, and it goes out of my mind."

"It's all right if one of us remembers."

"It's better if both of us do. Peter, do you want some more children?"

What? Did I forget again? He drew a deep breath as his daughter snuggled against his chest.

"I do if you do. Can't be too much love in the world." Then he said, "Why? Are we going to have another one soon?"

Pia laughed, making her breasts jiggle. She was still feeding Melody, and she was bigger on top than she'd been when he found her sleeping in the forest. Peter had had to transfer his favourite pixie grip to her hand at night, to avoid waking in a pool of milk. He'd been looking forward to getting those breasts back for his own exclusive delight, but he was never going to say so.

"Oh, your face!" Pia yelped.

"Are we?" He fixed a happy expression. It wasn't difficult. He loved his miss and their little miss. He could easily love another little miss, too.

"No, darling Peter, we're not. At least, not yet. I want Melody to have her time, and she has to be *aside* from me before I can give fair time to another baby. Besides, I want to give *you* time. I would like to give you an oh fuck friendly."

"Pia! Language!"

"You know what I mean." She gestured towards his groin.

"You want to do the first one?"

"Yes."

"You don't want—" He felt bereft. He loved holding her and giving her exactly what she needed by supporting her at the proper angle.

"Darling Peter, of course, I want. But when we do that you have to keep some of your mind for holding. You can only have the oh fuck moments when you don't have to think of that."

He remembered the utter bliss of not having to think of that. He hadn't had to think of it when Pia was carrying Melody, but he'd had to be careful in other ways, and he'd been always aware of the changes in her body.

He remembered the way humans did such things. Those stupid, horrible things Barbie had made him use. He hadn't had to remember to hold, but they'd felt dreadful. He put the things, and Barbie, out of his mind. They belonged to that other part of his life when he'd tried, just for a while, to *live human*. Inevitably, he thought of old man Thaddeus Appledore.

Poor old geezer. Wonder what happened to that set of swan pictures? He was happy with that. Proud.

He came back to his perfect present, with his two favourite people in the world.

"Can I have that friendly now?"

"Not now . . . I'm going to have tea and cake with Mum and Alba. I'll feed Melody, and then they're going to have her for her long sleep and give her some fun and that fruit mash Mum makes when she wakes up. We'll go and fetch her home for her supper."

Peter sorted through his decidedly mixed feelings about that. On the one hand, he longed to have Pia to himself, just for a while. On the other, he was displeased at the thought of other folk, even the ebullient Tess Tillien and her kindly daughter, Alba, having his daughter's company without him and Pia.

"Dad's longing to know her better, too. He was so glad we had a miss. He says he doesn't know anything about lads, although he was one himself."

"Melody looks like me," Peter said.

"I know that."

"Your dad doesn't like me much."

Pia giggled. "Oh, you'll never forgive him for that grilling he gave you when you first met him, will you? He does like you, and you ought to know that by now. He just needed to be sure you were a fit man for his miss."

"Huh."

"You are the best and only man for this miss, and Dad knows that." Pia twirled. "Do you think I could look like this if I wasn't the happiest miss in the world?"

Peter looked at her gleaming hair and her satiny skin. She was the most beautiful miss he'd ever seen, and she was all his.

Occasionally he had bad dreams about green-willied fuckers trying to get her away from him, but he knew better than to *go pixie* when he was awake.

Anyhow, she wouldn't go with them. She likes me. No green-willied fucker could possibly take her if she didn't want to go.

So, that was all right.

"Melody and I are going to take tea with the Tillien ladies, and then when Dad gets back from fixing whatever he's fixing, I'll come back home."

"How long will you be?"

"I would suppose about three hours." Pia pursed her lips. "You should probably go to the manse and find Peter G. We haven't seen him for a while. Make sure he knows we love him."

"You love Peter G?"

"Yes, you numpty. I love Peter G. He's a darling lad and your best friend, and he's Melody's godfather . . . and your godson. Why wouldn't I love him? He's like the little brother

I never got to have. Go and do something with him, without me. Be lads together. Then come home, and we'll have that oh fuck friendly."

Peter debated with himself and came to a conclusion. It was going to be Pia's way or no way. He kissed his drowsy daughter affectionately. "Right, Melody, you go and visit. Be good. Let your fucking fix-it grandad see what a lovely miss I got on my miss."

"Language, Peter."

Peter laughed. He was pleased with the world.

After his wife and daughter left, he went to the manse. There were several people in the parlour, including his grandmother, Clover, and a braeside lassie who was heavy with child. He raised a hand in greeting and slipped off to Berryman Grene's study, where he came upon another braeside lassie, a tall, full-figured woman with brown hair and eyes like autumn leaves. She was holding the red cat, Rory Inkersoll's mani-self, with such love that he guessed she must be Mistress Emer Drumwiddy.

Peter gazed at her appreciatively. She was glorious. She was also nothing like his Pia. If Rory Inkersoll loved this woman, he would never want Pia any more than Peter wanted this buxom beauty.

Better not stare too much, though. Might get clawed.

He moved his attention to his grandfather. "Greet you, Grandad. Where's Peter G?"

"Gone to Russet, who's looking for him, as usual. What have you done with Pia?"

"Taking tea with Melody and Granny Tess."

Better go and be polite to Aunt Russet.

Peter dashed off. He caught up with Peter G a little way from the manse. "Peter G!"

His cousin turned to face him.

"You've grown again," Peter observed.

"You keep saying that."

"I know. Listen, Pete, are you all right? Pia's worried that we haven't seen you."

Peter G looked up at him. "I'm not really all right, but I'm trying to be."

Peter held out his arms. "Want a hug?"

"What? From you?"

"Yes, from me. I'm a dad now, but you were the first baby I ever hugged. You taught me how to do it so I could hug my little miss properly." He smiled, remembering. "Do you know I was the first pixie man to ever hold you after Uncle Quercus and your grandads?"

"I didn't know that."

"So, I can hug you. *No harm.*"

His cousin's face wobbled, and he stepped forward. Peter hugged him. "What have you been doing to yourself, Pete?"

"I told Gentie we couldn't keep borrowing time."

Peter had never understood his cousin's friendship with the person he called Gentie, but he thought he'd better try.

Melody might need me to understand something sometime.

"Gentie's your friend, I know. What else can you tell me about her?"

"She's a pixie miss."

"Good. *Good.* You can be friends with a pixie miss and wed one, too. They understand things a lot better than humans."

"She's eight, like me."

"Eight, eh? Are you only eight?"

"You know I am. So, it's not like Master Rory having to wait and wait. He's—"

"He's just wed Mistress Drumwiddy. I know. I saw them just now . . . only she was holding the red cat. Fucking odd, but I hope they'll be happy."

"But Gentie's *not* like that. Not a grown lady. She's like me."

"Then what's the trouble?" Peter asked, mystified.

"I don't want to wed her, or . . . you know, do private

things with her."

"I should fucking hope not! She's a child! If anyone started wanting to do private things with my little miss . . . Fuck me. I'd have something to say about that!" He pulled himself together. "So, what do you want to do with her, Pete?"

"I want to play with her. You know, swim, maybe learn to play the guitar, like Joe can, and show her your goats. We could cook stuff and climb the rocks behind the falls."

"Sounds good to me. Who's Joe?"

"Joe Bakewell. He's mostly human, but a bit pixie, too. His grandad's Portier Grene—Grandad Grene's cousin."

"Oh, *that* Joe. Betula's boy. What's he doing *over here* then?"

"Being sponsored, of course. Only it's more like visiting, because he goes home a lot. He has to go to school *over there*."

"Nice lad, is he?"

"I like him. He's ten."

Peter felt a slight pang. His friend had made other friends. *That's good. Good. He needs friends closer to his own age.*

"So, what about your friend Gentie?" he prompted.

"I haven't met her yet. She has *the sight,* and she borrowed time with me so we could meet in the white place. That's what Master Rory says. And I told her we couldn't keep doing it, and I miss her."

"Fuck, that must hurt. But you did the right thing."

"How do you know?"

"Because you *always* do the right thing. That's why we made you Melody's godfather. You know how to do the right thing, so when she gets older, you can tell her if she's going wrong. I should have helped you with this before, as I'm your godfather. You said Master Rory gave you some advice?"

Peter G nodded against Peter's chest.

Again, Peter struggled with jealousy.

"That's *fine.* Rory Inkersoll's an odd cuss, but he's a good man. I helped him once with a little bit of stuff he wanted to know, so now he's helped you." He closed his arms in a squeeze and then gently withdrew so he could see his cousin's face. "Pete, it's an odd old world, but friends are good, even if you can't keep them forever. Loving's good, if it does no harm. Did you know I loved a human maid before I knew Pia?"

"Was that Barbie? The one you lived with *over there*?"

"Yes. She told me she never wanted to hear from me again."

"Did you do something wrong?"

"No. Neither did she. We just weren't *right* together. She knew that, but I was too silly to know until she yelled at me."

"Maybe you ought to tell her you're happy now," Peter G said.

"I would if I knew where she was. I hope she's happy, too. Anyway, you did the right thing with your friend Gentie. You've lost her for now, but you wouldn't want to have never known her, would you?"

"No," Peter G said in a small voice. "Would you want to have never known Barbie?"

That's a hard one.

He thought of the misery knowing Barbie had brought him, but he also thought of the interesting things. He'd learned to drive, and he'd got to know Judit Creed. Old Thadd had been an interesting person to talk to, and he'd quite enjoyed posing for different artists. He'd liked Johnny Hanover even though the man had been far too interested in pixie blood.

"I'm glad I knew her. It let me find out what life I really want," he said finally. "There was an old man I was friends with, too, and he showed me that sometimes you can't get what you want, but if you're nice about it, you can get something else."

"How do you mean?"

"Well. He was an old geezer, and he was a gaylord. You know what that means?"

Peter G looked puzzled.

"It's a man who likes to do private things with other men instead of with maids. There are gay maids, too, so it works out fine *over here.*

"*Over there,* though, that's not something people want you to be. This nice old geezer wanted to lie down with me, but I'm not a gaylord, so I said *no.*"

Actually, he'd said, *not fucking likely.*

"And he was nice about that?"

"Yes, he said, *all right, I'm disappointed, but it was worth asking.* And because he was so nice, I used to hug him now and then. I think that was what he *really* wanted, being an old geezer."

Even as he said that he wondered if it made sense. When *he* was an old geezer, wouldn't he still want friendlies with his miss?

He got back to the point. "So, you've lost Gentie for a bit, but you have this human mix friend now, and that must fill a bit of the gap for you."

"Yes. We get to do a lot of the things I like, though we don't go dancing."

"You could. The braeside laddies dance, and the leppys do. They'll dance with anyone, even their grandfathers. Fucking odd of them."

"Wouldn't you?"

"Fecking hell no! Grandad Berry's too vicarish and Grandad Alexis is too scary. It'd be like dancing with myself in a mirror."

Peter G laughed, which was what Peter had intended. He said encouragingly, "And you might meet your Gentie properly one day. In fact, you're practically bound to!"

"Are you sure?"

"Of course! You said she'd been borrowing time, and she'll have to pay it back. She can't do that if she never meets you."

Peter wondered if what he'd just said made any sense at all. Apparently, it did, because Peter G's eyes widened.

"Pia and Melody have gone to have tea with Tess and Alba. Do you want to come swimming with me?"

"Yes."

Peter conjured a drying cloth from the cottage. "Oh, better get one for—Fuck me!" He stared as a large cloth suddenly eclipsed Peter G.

His cousin uttered a bleat of fright and fought his way out of the folds. "What did you do that for?"

Peter laughed at him. "I didn't. You did. Fuck me. You can conjure! At *eight!*"

Peter G's mouth opened, and Peter rubbed his curly hair in congratulation. "Let's go swimming, pixie man."

Peter spent a couple of hours splashing in the falls pool and watching Peter G's studied concentration as he conjured a few small items. The waterfolk waved cheerfully but left them be, satisfied that they were quite happy amusing themselves.

When their skin began to wrinkle, they got out and dried in the sun. Peter G tried and failed to dress himself, and Peter chuckled. "That takes a while to get right. You can't mess with anyone else's clothes, either. You do know that, right?"

Peter G rolled his eyes. "You can only do that if you're *very* close, and who you can do it with changes over time. Mum can't do my clothes anymore, not since I was five."

"Right." Peter glanced at the sun.

So did Peter G. A chagrined look spread over his face. "I was supposed to go home after I left the manse."

"And *I* was supposed to send you home. Instead, we've been having fun. Never mind, tell Aunt Russet it's my fault you're late."

"I will. She'll believe me, too. She thinks most things are your fault."

Peter chuckled and watched his cousin depart at speed. Then he set off for the cottage, warm with anticipation.

CHAPTER SIXTEEN: OXYTOCIN

The Cottage, Pixie Forest. 1952
Peter Peckerdale

Pia wasn't there, but Peter knew she'd come soon. He pottered about, making tea and eating new peas in the garden, sharing the pods with his goats. He picked some flowers and stuffed them in a mug on the little table.

The door swung open, and he turned slowly.

"Greet you, Master Peckerdale."

"Greet you, Mistress Peckerdale. Is our miss all right?"

"Mistress Melody is asleep in Alba's bed. Mum will send a note if she needs us."

"She won't send any notes," Peter said.

"No, probably not. She told me to be sure to get some rest. You know she'll look after Melody as if she was her own."

Peter said, "I made tea."

"I've had some. Did you?"

"Yes. Had mine while I was waiting."

They eyed one another, and then Pia flicked her fingers, and her clothing vanished. She turned slowly and ran her hands down her sides before cupping her breasts and squeezing experimentally. "I gave our miss a good feed."

"So, I can play with them?"

He took a step forward.

"Yes, all you like. But first, we're going to have an *oh fuck* friendly. Get into bed, Master Peckerdale."

Peter shed his clothes and got into bed. Pia got in with him, and they rolled together and kissed. He pressed urgently against her. "Fuck, I'm going to—"

"Control yourself. You are not going to spill yet. You want that friendly, don't you?"

"Yes." He wanted it so badly he couldn't manage more than one syllable.

"Lie down then, and you may have it." She wriggled out of his arms. "And remember, I want you to focus on your willy. Don't worry about me. I'll have mine when you're able to concentrate."

He caught his breath as she took him in a confident grasp and ran her fingers down his length.

"Nice and big," she said.

He didn't answer.

She kissed him, and he jerked wildly in response.

Pia's hand came down to squeeze his thigh. "Slow down, darling Peter. Let me tend to you." Her lips closed and she ran her tongue over him. After a moment, she started sucking slowly.

The urgency went away and he relaxed, floating into bliss. He reached down and rubbed her back, enjoying the softness of her skin.

Her hand left his thigh, and she cupped it around his balls, sucking harder.

His breath came faster. "Oh—oh—oh *fuck*, that's good."

He felt her giggle against him and smiled in response.

"Oh *fuck*, that's fucking lovely," he said. "Fuck me, that's—oh—" He felt the unmistakable gathering of immanent spurting and tried to hold back. "Wait—"

In response, she sucked harder and harder.

It was no good. He had to let go. *"Oh, fuck-oh fuck-oh—"* He jerked in the bed and lost his train of thought as everything cut loose. "Oh!"

She patted his thigh reassuringly and went on sucking,

gently, dreamily, as he came down.

Finally, she let him go and kissed him with a full-blown pixie smooch. Then she moved up into his arms and said brightly, "Now *that* was a grand *oh fuck* friendly. There's no hurry, but when you're ready, I want you to smooch me down there."

"Smooch? Not lick?"

"Smooch. Maybe stick your finger in."

Really? Still, if that's what she wants . . .

He kissed her gratefully. "I love you, my miss."

"I know. I love you, too. Do you feel good?"

He tried to formulate a way of telling her how good he felt. "I feel *half* good," he said at last.

"Only half?"

"I'll feel all good when I give you what you gave me."

"Oh! Better get on with it, then."

He moved down the bed and kissed her belly and thighs. She wriggled impatiently.

Here goes. He configured his lips for kissing and brought his mouth dead centre, kissing her with real affection. She squirmed, panting, and he remembered her other request. He settled on his middle finger and very gently pushed it inside.

She moaned urgently, and her hand came down to grasp his hair.

He explored a little, enjoying the elastic feeling. She moaned again, and he deepened the kiss, passing his free hand under her to lift her to her preferred angle.

Almost immediately, he felt a hard squeeze on his finger. It slackened, squeezed again, slackened, and then closed so hard his finger slid in full length.

She cried out, and he was almost alarmed in case he was hurting her. He felt a gush of warmth and squirmed with embarrassment, but there was no time to think of that now.

He gentled his lips to little kisses and then turned his cheek to rest on her, waiting patiently until he could reclaim his finger.

Finally, she released the pressure, and he heard her gasping for breath. He withdrew gently and kissed her belly again.

"You're so fucking gorgeous."

She tugged on his hair. "Come up and say that to my face."

He came up and smoothed her tumbled hair. "You're all sticky. Sweaty."

"I feel as if I'd run to Fiddletown and back. That was —"

He kissed her chin. "You're so fucking gorgeous."

"Sticky and sweaty?"

"That, too."

She chuckled.

Peter said, "It was as well that was my finger and not my willy."

"Oh?"

"Fuck, if that had been my willy, I'd *never* have thought of holding."

She nudged him with her knee. "Ick. You didn't hold even then, did you?"

"No. Sorry. I hoped you hadn't noticed that." He'd spilled again, transported when she cried out.

"No need to be sorry." She wriggled up the bed and brought his head to her breast. "If you feel like a little snuggle there, I'll try not to spill Melody's supper."

He felt the dampness under his cheek. "You already did."

"Hm. I wonder why?"

"I expect it's oxytocin." He brought out the word with pride.

"What?"

"Barbie's brother was a medical student. He told me about hormones and things, and he said that one has a lot of *clinical effects.*"

"*Clinical effects?*" She sounded outraged.

He shrugged and kissed her breast. "When you feed our

134

miss, it feels good, right?"

"Ye-es. It stings for a second, the way it prickles when you're about to cry. Then it feels good. That's when she stops pulling and starts sucking slowly and swallowing."

"Oxytocin is a *let go* hormone. It helps you let go the milk and feel good while Melody gets her supper."

"Oh."

"It also lets go down there, I expect."

"The things you know."

He sucked the nipple gently. "I don't want a mouthful. Oh, mm, fuck . . ."

Pia pulled his ear. "You stop that. I didn't."

"No, you didn't." He rolled his face against her. "I don't remember sucking from Mum."

"*Peter!*"

"Sorry. Just saying."

She sighed. "Peter, I've been thinking about Barbie."

"Mm? So have I."

"*Why?*" She sounded cross.

"Peter G asked something about her. He said I ought to let her know I hope she's happy."

"Maybe you should."

He sucked again, enjoying the tingles the action gave him.

"Did you do that with her?" Pia asked.

Peter raised his head. "Fuck, no! She said it was . . . no. I never gave her an *oh fuck me* friendly, either. She wouldn't let me."

"Just what did you do?"

"Kissing. Cuddling. Some not-so-friendlies with a rubber."

"What's a rubber?"

"Like a sock you put over your willy to catch everything, so you don't start a baby. Humans can't *hold*."

Pia picked up his limp willy with her finger and thumb. "Maybe we need to get some rubber socks."

135

"No. Please. They're horrible. She even made me blow one up to make sure it didn't have holes. Tasted fucking terrible. I made her blow up the next one, and after that, she didn't want to either."

"Did you ever do it without a rubber sock?"

"No. We didn't do it much even with one. She's fun, but she just wasn't into *that*. She thought it was wrong."

"So she never sucked your willy." Pia waggled her captive.

"Shit, no!"

She closed her hand on it. "Good. *Good*. Because that willy is mine, and no one, *no one* ever gets to touch it but me. Oh, except you, of course, when you shake off the drips after a pisserfall. Or if you ever need to help yourself."

"I don't do that anymore."

"Never? What about when I was sore after having Melody?"

He said, "I didn't do it. I wanted to make my two misses safe and happy. I didn't think about *that*."

She said, "Next time we have a baby, remind me you need tending, too. Even if I'm sore and I don't want to be touched down there, I can still look after you."

"You don't need to."

"I *want* to. Don't you get it? I *love* doing that. You taste lovely, and when you stop jerking and just lie there, waves of happiness come off you. It's like swimming in sunshine, and I'm the one making it happen. And then you just gush out, and that's like biting into an orange. It makes me happy to do that for you."

He remembered his blissful feeling when she gripped his finger and half saw what she meant.

"All right. But I'll have to do something for you."

"Just say *oh fuck* a lot. That makes me feel *valued*."

"You don't like it when I say that. You say, *Language, Peter*."

"There's a time and a place for everything." She gave his willy another good squeeze, let go, and pulled him closer. "We have another couple of hours before Melody needs her supper. Can I snuggle under your chin?"

He laughed and made the necessary adjustments. "We'll need a wash before we go to get our little miss."

"Mm. Peter?"

"Yes?"

"You should send a message to Barbie."

"I don't know where she is."

"We'll find out. Do you know where her brother is?"

"His name's Johnny Hanover. He was at Appledore Hospital. Maybe he still is."

"You should go and see him."

Peter thought about going *over there*. He didn't feel enthusiastic. He'd never been back since he'd fled after Barbie left.

Pia kissed his chest. "We've never been dancing."

"What? No . . . we can go to a cèilidh if you like, or the midsummer ball at the manor. Take Peter G. He wants to dance, but not with Joe Bakewell."

"Yes, we'll do that. We can take Melody, too, because there are plenty of people to hold her. But what I mean was, we've never been dancing *over there*."

"No." He wondered where this was leading.

"I'd like to. I have human friends I haven't seen since I was sponsored. I'd like to go and see them again, but before you *go pixie* on me, I want you to come with me. I expect some of them have boyfriends or husbands and we could have some fun. We could take Alba with us . . . she should have been sponsored by now, but she's been holding back."

He wanted to say they could have fun at the cottage, in bed, but he remembered what she'd said about hoarding. "Okay. Let's. We can go to Patterdale, maybe. It's closer to the gateway than Appledore. Or we might go and see Prue, or even

Judit Creed, if she's still at the art school. She was going to get a house with her man." He thought of something else. "Joe Bakewell is a kind of cousin of mine and Peter G's. He's been coming to spend time here. His dad's human, and we might get him or Joe's mum to lend us a car. Otherwise, we'd have to get Prue to come and get us."

"You can drive?"

"Yes. Barbie taught me in Johnny's car, and I used to borrow old Thadd's." He winced, remembering the last time he'd borrowed it. The old man was gone, Barbie was gone, and he'd been desperate to get home. He'd appropriated Thadd's car one last time and driven to the open pasture where the copse of trees concealed the pixie forest gateway.

I should have got someone to drive me or told someone to take the car back.

"Have you got a — whatever it's called?" Pia asked.

"Licence? Well, I did have. Might have fucking lapsed by now. They might be after me about that old car." He frowned, but interest was stirring. "Would Alba feel better about being sponsored if you and I went to see her, say, once a week?"

"I'm sure she would. I went to a friend of Mum's, and she'll take Alba, too."

"Okay."

Pia giggled. "Okay? You talking like a human now?"

"It comes back to me. I'll get Peter G to see what Joe Bakewell says."

If Pia thought it odd that they needed to get information from an eight-year-old and a ten-year-old, she didn't say so. She let the subject drop and kissed Peter's neck, rubbing against him. After a while, she put her hand on his willy again. "Peter?"

"Mm?"

"If we have another friendly, do you promise to hold back?"

"Yes. I already spurted twice."

"So maybe you don't really want another?"

For answer, he rolled her onto her back and conjured a pillow down under her hips. "Stop me if it hurts."

"It won't." She put her arms around him and parted her legs. "Come in me and then don't move."

"Don't move?"

She giggled again, breathlessly. "I want to see what we can do with a pixie smooch."

He pressed in carefully. Despite Melody's birth, it was still a tight fit. It felt wonderful.

"You didn't say *oh fuck*," Pia said much later, as they still lay joined in the bed.

"Couldn't. Had my mouth busy. I was *oh fucking* in my mind."

That was only partly true, as he'd been more attuned to Pia's pleasure.

He moved away from her. "We'd better get washed and go and get our miss."

Pia got up reluctantly. "Quick wash then, and . . . Peter, I think Mum and Dad would like to have Melody for a few hours every week."

Peter said, "It would be good for her to get used to being with other people."

"Yes. But I was thinking it would be good for me to be with my favourite person."

"Going dancing *over there*."

She bent and kissed him. "Yes, sometimes, but mostly right here in our bed."

Chapter Seventeen: Trust

Judit Creed hooked her arm around the smooth pole, swung in a circle, and then posed with one high-heeled shoe propped playfully against her knee. Her full skirt dropped back, revealing a long split that ended mid-thigh. She lifted her head and stretched one arm in a ballet curve.

"Take it off, Missus!"

Judit tossed her head. "Control yourself, soldier."

She swung again and used her free hand to untie the ribbon at the top of her blouse. She pulled it very, very slowly.

"Don't keep us in suspenders! Show us the goods!"

"Soldier. I won't warn you again."

She pulled the ribbon free, let go of the pole and made herself into a cross-shape, holding the ribbon stretched high above her head. She held the pose for a moment and then stretched down to touch the floor.

The audience applauded.

Judit flattened her hands and lifted one foot and then the other, rising into a handstand before she came down into a backbend, straightened, and bowed.

Shrill whistles rang out, and Judit grinned and ruffled her hair. She coiled up the ribbon from her blouse and tossed one end into the crowd.

Her aim was good, and the lanky man she'd had to discipline caught the weighted end and hung on. She drew it slowly back towards her, bringing him with it, and kissed him on the cheek.

"Hang on to this, soldier. Might keep you company," she said and ducked back through the curtain.

A few minutes later, he came around the back of the stage to meet her.

"Tommy, what am I going to do with you?"

Tommy Creed gave her back her ribbon. "Can't resist it, Jude. All those other fellers drooling over you turns me on."

"Everything turns you on. Clear out. I've got to get changed."

"I'll come with you."

"Don't you want to watch Corinna do her set?"

"Who?"

"Corinna Connemara . . . Irish, I think."

"Don't know her. Is she any good?"

"Better than me."

"No one is better than you."

"She can tie herself into knots, and she's bigger up top. Still, I have my admirers."

He took her hand, and they went to the dressing room.

A dark-haired woman in a kimono looked up from doing her make-up at the mirror. "You again. Have to report you to the management," she said to Tommy and winked.

She laid aside her powder puff. "I'm on with Corinna. See you, kids."

"Bye, Muriel."

Muriel took off the kimono, revealing black stockings and a short skater's dress, stepped into her shoes, and swayed out the door. Tommy locked it behind her.

Judit put her hands on her hips. "Sure you don't want to watch Corinna and Mu? I think they'll work in a cuddle. They're not really that way, but they pretend."

"I don't want to watch other girls when I can watch you."

Judit unclipped three press-studs at her hip and let her full knickers fall to the ground. She hoisted herself onto the dressing room bench and eyed her husband with enjoyment. "Atten-shun!"

"Been at attention since you started your set."

She beckoned him closer and pulled down his zipper. "Let's see . . . ten, and you're out."

"Awww. Fifteen?"

"Ten. Or would you rather wear a rubber?" She patted his crotch. "I'll bring you off properly at home."

He pressed into her. "One."

"Two," she said.

"Three."

"Slow down. You're getting too excited." She put her arms around him. "What did you tell your mum you were doing?"

"Catching up on business. She said if we were late, she'd put Tolly and Tad to bed at her place."

"Are you sure she doesn't mind?"

"No. I told her we might go over to the new place and measure up for curtains if you finished on time."

He moved again. "One."

Judit said, "You lost count. When do you reckon, we can move in?"

"Maybe next week. Now, where were we . . . One."

"Five . . . no, six."

"That wasn't a move."

"It was a move. Do you want to wear a rubber?"

"No," he said meekly. He swayed forward. "Seven . . ."

"Eight."

"Maybe we can move in sooner. Seven."

"Nine."

He groaned. "Oh, Jude."

"Ten. Out you get. Tell you what, I'll put on a private show for you tonight."

He kissed her. "That almost makes up for . . . oooh."

"That's eleven! Out."

She slid down from the bench, resumed her knickers and put on her coat. "Let's go."

He zipped up reluctantly and took her arm. "You know you don't have to go on working here if you don't want to, Jude. I'm bringing in enough, and the old man's money gave us the house."

"I like working here." She looked up at him. "That solicitor came round earlier."

"What, again?"

"Yes. You know that swansong painting Thadd was working on just before he passed?"

"I know of it. Never saw it. Is it any good?"

"Hard to say. I just pose for 'em. Don't have to appreciate 'em."

"Must have been a big one. He had you tied up for weeks on it."

"I was glad of the rest. Taddy took it out of me a bit."

"Rest?"

"I spent a lot of time curled artistically on a whopping great velvet cushion. Even when I had to get into the *woe is me I'm about to be rogered by a swan* pose, Thadd had a kind of frame set up for me to lean on. The draperies covered the sides. He was good like that."

Tommy opened the door of the car for her. "The old coot was always good to you. To us."

"He was. He might have been that way, but he had a kind heart."

The engine started. "Wonder if your rogering swan will ever show up to claim his property?" Tommy patted the wooden dashboard, which he kept lovingly polished.

"About that . . . that was one of the things the solicitor chappie wanted, aside from talking about the painting. He had a letter from young Peter, hand-delivered by a doctor at the hospital, of all things."

"Really? Did you find out where he dashed off to?"

"He doesn't say. He was seeing Barbie Hanover, who used to hang about the art school. She did some of the vanilla modelling when they wanted a bit more up top than I've got."

"You've got plenty."

"Yes, about as much as a broomstick. Barbie was a nice kid, but a bit of a prude. Anyhow, not long after the old man died, they had a bust-up, and Barbie took off. Peter did, too . . . in the car." She, too, patted the dashboard. "Well, he had every right. It turned up miles away, near some trees. Key still in it."

Tommy turned to stare at her. "You never told me any of this."

"I didn't know myself, then. I was expecting, remember? Apart from a few tummy poses, the art school didn't want me, so I didn't get to hear the gossip. Anyhow, the boarding house chased up some woman who did the booking for Peter . . . got him the room, I mean."

"His mum? His fancy woman?"

"Don't know that he had a fancy woman. He was big and sexy. Swore like a navvy, but he was innocent, somehow. Used to talk about Barbie all the time."

"Country boy," Tommy diagnosed.

"Could be. Green." She giggled.

"What?"

"He really was green, a bit. You know, down there."

Tommy said, "Tell me more."

"Tall, well set up, eyes sort of turquoise, big hands. Very limber. He could hold poses in the natural that make me hurt after thirty seconds. Twist himself into a plait, almost."

"And green down there?"

"Well, I couldn't help noticing. When I was cringing and he was looming, it dangled."

"I've got to see this painting."

"Maybe you will. There's been a bit of argy-bargy about who it belongs to. Depends on whether it's a chattel or an asset or something, but it looks like it's being cleared up soon, and when it is, there's going to be a retrospective of the old man's work. When the paintings are sold, the money goes into the estate."

"So, you might be in for more cash?"

"No need to be greedy, Tommy."

"I'm not, but it helps if we can plan ahead a bit. The old man liked you, and it's not as if you did anything smarmy."

"No, it was straight up. The old dear liked to talk. Used to ask about you and Tolly and all. I suppose we might get a couple of hundred quid. I thought if we did, we might make a trust for the kiddies."

"Good notion. Would this solicitor set it up?"

"I don't know. Depends." She mused for a while, and then said, "He wanted to know if I knew where to contact Peter because he's never claimed his chunk of the money. It's just sitting with some bank or stockbroker, nest-egging. He's in line for a share of the painting money, too. Of course, I said I had no idea where he is. He never talked about where he came from, just about Barbie. Oh, and he talked to the old man about pictures and people he'd known. He was fond of him, I think. Not that way."

"Why did they think you'd know where he was?"

"Clutching at straws. Back when he left, the woman who arranged things for Peter said she didn't know where he'd gone, exactly, and she couldn't get in touch unless he did first. She told 'em where the car might be, though, and it was there."

"That letter doesn't say anything useful? What about the postmark?" Tommy changed gear and turned into the street where their new house stood, smelling of sawdust.

"Johnny, that's Barbie's brother, said the letter just turned up. No postmark and no stamp. No one saw who delivered it. The solicitor chappie said it authorises him to deal with the banker or broker or whoever it is. Got the keys?"

"What do you think?" Tommy helped her out of the car and jingled the car keys. Then he pushed the bunch against her waist.

"Now what?" Judit said.

"Just unlocking the chastity belt."

"Didn't you do that at work?"

"Did I? I did not. You mean some don Juan has had his wicked way with you?"

"Only eleven strokes worth."

"That's all right then. That doesn't count." He took her arm, and they went into the new house. Tommy stopped her and pulled a black scarf out of his coat pocket.

"What is that?"

"Got a surprise for you."

"You know I'm not into kinky stuff."

"Not kinky. Turn around." She turned, and he bound the scarf around her eyes. "Right-o. Now walk forward. I won't let you fall."

"I know you won't." She trusted him utterly unless counting was involved.

"Keep walking. Door. Right, now three steps. Ready?"

She stopped and raised her hands to the blindfold.

"Just hold on a bit, honey." He rustled about.

"What's that smell? Like in a church."

"Hold on . . . oh, and you might want to take off your coat. Just drop it where you are."

Puzzled, she complied.

"All right. Take the scarf off."

She undid the bow at the back and blinked a few times in the uneven light.

Candles.

She exclaimed with delight at the sight of a double bed scattered with rose petals. A small table held the candles and two champagne flutes along with a bottle. A tall pole mounted on a stand stood at the foot of the bed.

"Oh, Tommy!"

"Like it?" He grinned at her from the bed.

"I like it."

He hitched some pillows behind him and pulled out a piece of old towelling. "I'm ready for my private show. I even got a pole for you."

"Two poles." She nodded to his groin. She walked around to the tall pole and gave it an experimental shake. "Nice and solid. Ready, lover?"

"I'm always ready."

Judit gripped the pole in one hand and wrapped one leg about it. She leaned out and unclipped the studs to let her knickers fall. Then she started to dance.

Her husband watched appreciatively for a while, and then said, "How about a bit of attention for the other pole?"

Judit finished her routine unhurriedly and removed her heels. Then she put one knee on the bed and swung the other over Tommy. "Rubber or trust?"

"Trust."

"Promise to tell me in time?"

He said, "Promise."

She settled into position. "One."

"Two."

"Three."

"Four."

"Five."

"Three."

"Tommy!"

"Ouch!"

"Seven."

"You skipped one."

"Concentrate, then."

They made it to nineteen before Tommy said, "Jude."

She got off and curled beside him, grasping his wet cock in her hands. "Twenty."

"Twenty-one."

"Twenty — uh — "

"That's it, soldier. Give it to me all."

He groaned.

"At ease."

Judit went on holding him and then reached for the towelling and cleaned him up.

"You?"

She lay down, and he pulled her close and pushed his hand under her skirt. "You're so wet."

"Mm."

He kissed her, rubbing his thumb in lazy circles until she sighed.

"Better than a rubber," she said.

He wiped his hand on the cloth.

"I hope you've got another one of those for me."

"Can't you use the same one?"

"No. Might have baby-planters in it."

"In that case . . ." He pulled a new one out from under the pillow.

They lay together for a while with her head on his shoulder. Then Judit gestured towards the bottle and glasses. "Is this a special occasion?"

"Got a promotion."

"Oh, Tommy! You've only been out of the army for eighteen months!"

"Yes, but I'm giving satisfaction, as they say. So, your dancing money can go into the fund for the kids . . . what you don't spend on frillies."

"Since when do I buy frillies?"

"You don't. I wish you would."

"What, so you can leer at me?"

"No. I wish you could have more fun, that's all."

"I do have fun. I like dancing, and the other girls are good company. The people at the art school still get me in. Tell you what, I'll buy some glad rags for the retrospective when it happens. How's that? Something classy, so no one will recognise me as the model."

"I hope people do recognise you."

"What, with a man in his birthday suit looming over me?"

He nodded.

"Why on earth?"

Tommy seemed lost for words.

Judit nipped the skin of his thigh with her fingernails. "Give."

"Promise you won't get angry?"

"Am I likely to?"

"Most women would."

"I'm not most women. I'm your wife."

"Right." He sat up, pulled the cork and poured them each a glass of champagne. "Get that into you."

Judit obeyed, giggling as the bubbles burst and chilled her face. "Should have had this before."

"Might have lost count then."

"You did anyway. Go on."

He took her glass and put it with his on the table. "You know it turns me on to see you dance."

"Yes. And it turns you on to see other people watching me. The other girls think that's strange. Even the ones whose boyfriends first met them at the Cat say they get a bit funny about it once they think they have an exclusive."

"I just like to see their faces. I imagine how they feel and what they're imagining. I know it's a million miles from what I feel because they just see the dancer. I see my wife."

She said, "You don't want me to do it with anyone else, I hope. 'Cos I won't."

"No! I might daydream about it, but I don't want it to happen. I like to think of other people wanting you, though."

Judit shook her head at him. "You can think all you like, but it's not to go beyond thinking."

"It never would."

"So, you'd like us to turn up at this retrospective where people can see me in the painting with Peter . . . only it's not really Peter and me . . . and then know I'm with you and have them wonder. Is that it?"

"Yes."

"Let's, then. Pity Peter won't be there. I could give him a kiss and let them really wonder."

"You're not angry?"

"No. But don't go talking like that to your mates at the pub. I don't want them thinking they can put the hard word on me."

"I never would."

She indicated the bottle. "Bit more?"

He refilled the glasses.

Chapter Eighteen: Retrospective

The Gallery, Patterdale. 1955
Peter Peckerdale

Waiting for Prue to meet them at the gateway or borrowing a car for their jaunts *over there* was a nuisance, but Peter had hit on a way of having a vehicle available.

It was so simple, and he was amazed he hadn't thought of it before. One day, he and Pia left Melody with her delighted Tillien grandparents, went through the gateway and set off to walk into Patterdale, which was the nearest human settlement to the gateway. They had been there before, but not often, as they usually went to the larger town of Appledore where Peter knew his way around.

The walk took an unconscionably long time since they had to take the linear route along the road and not *go* as they could at home. They were about halfway, by Peter's reckoning, when a car horn tooted behind them.

"Great bogle!" Pia jumped and clutched at his hand.

Peter had been enjoying the sunshine and his miss's conversation, and he scowled at the interruption.

"Better see what they want," Pia said.

Still scowling, Peter turned to where the car had pulled in a few yards behind them. It looked vaguely familiar.

A man stuck his head out of the window. "Want a lift, mate?"

Peter stared at him. From the bit he could see, the man was lanky, with brown hair and freckled skin. He'd never seen

151

him before.

Human.

His hand tightened on Pia's as a surge of jealousy rose. He shoved it down. "We're all right, thanks. Enjoying the walk."

"Please yourself."

The passenger side door opened and a woman got out. She was small, with fair hair like a courtfolk woman, and dark eyes. She leaned back in to speak to the driver and then twisted to look at Peter and Pia.

Something twinged in Peter's memory, just as the woman came forward in a rush. "Peter!"

Pia stepped away, and the woman gave the startled Peter a quick hug. "As I live and breathe, it's Peter!"

Peter stepped back. "Judit?"

"The same. Reckon you don't recognise me with my clothes on." She gave him an impish look and turned to Pia. "Hello. That came out all wrong. Peter and I used to work together at the art school." She turned and beckoned vigorously, and the man got out of the car and came towards them, grinning.

He held out a hand. "Tommy Creed. You'll be the looming swan."

Pia said, "Peter," in that tone she had, and Peter hastily took the offered hand.

"Peter Peckerdale. This is my miss, Pia. My wife, I mean," he added, remembering where they were. He added, "Pia, this is Judit, the maid who posed for Thadd's swan picture with me. I suppose this is her man."

"Been married for ten years," Tommy Creed said placidly. "Two kiddies, Tolly and Tad."

"We have a miss. Melody," Peter said.

Tommy said, "Where are you headed?"

"Into Patterdale," Pia said.

"So are we. You're welcome to a lift."

"Are you going to the retrospective, too?" Judit asked.

Peter dredged in his memory for the term. He was sure he'd heard it during his time working for the art teachers. "That means a kind of show?" he hazarded.

"Old Mister Appledore's paintings are being shown at the gallery. Some that were sold years ago are being borrowed, and then there's a sale of the ones he had in storage. It's a big thing."

"The old geezer came back into fashion," Tommy said.

"Pity people weren't this pleased with him when he was alive." Judit reached for Peter's hand. "Peter, I always hoped I'd see you again to say how pleased I was to hear you'd been with him when he passed. I know it upset you a lot." She broke off, and Peter scowled, biting his lip and remembering his misery.

Barbie. That night.

"Do you know where Barbie is?" he asked abruptly.

Judit glanced at Pia.

"I know about Barbie. She was his girlfriend for a while. I'm his forever wife," Pia said.

"That's a good way to look at it, Missus . . . um—"

"Pia."

"Pia. I haven't seen or heard from Barbie since she left in a hurry just about the time you did, Peter. Her brother, Johnny, was at the hospital, remember? He was there until a couple of years ago . . ."

"He left in fifty-three. That was when they started talking about the retrospective," Tommy said.

"That's right. I haven't kept in touch with either of them, so sorry, can't help you."

Peter shrugged. He and Pia had decided to check on Barbie when Melody was a baby, but it had never happened. He could have gone to the hospital, but the place smelled wrong, and he couldn't forget the long hours waiting for old Thadd to go to glory. He'd conjured a letter there, hoping Johnny still had the same locker.

"They're showing the Swansong," Judit said. She glanced back to Pia and explained, "That was the big triple canvas Peter and I posed for back in nineteen fifty. It's a classical subject and a bit rude."

"Never laid eyes on it before. I'm going to leer at it and have people envying me for being with the model," Tommy said.

Peter shot him a startled look.

Pia poked him in the ribs. "Not all men are like you, you numpty. Not that you haven't got a lot better." She turned her attention to Tommy. "Peter hasn't ever seen this painting either, so we'd love to come. Are we dressed all right?"

Peter was wearing britches and a shirt, and Pia had on a long gold tunic that came to her toes. Peter now perceived Judit had a full blue dress with a sapphire necklace and earrings. "You look fucking nice," he said, remembering how Pia and his mother liked to be complimented.

Pia sighed. "Language, Peter."

"Sorry."

Judit giggled. "That's the Peter, I remember. So glad you haven't changed, dear. Glad you're married, too. And you both look lovely. I'm only got up in my glad rags because Tommy fancied having me look like a lady of means."

"You *are* a lady of means, thanks to old Thaddeus." Tommy turned to Peter. "Peter, did you get that solicitor chappie sorted out?"

Peter wished he hadn't come. At home at the cottage, he was comfortable and settled as a pixie man with a miss and a little miss, and everything he needed. He was someone, and he fitted into his place. *Over here* he felt himself slipping back to the awkward lad who'd messed up *living human.*

Judit said, "It's all right, Peter. Nothing was wrong. He'd

just got a letter from you and wanted to talk to you about the paintings and finances."

"I told him to let Den Porthwellian look after it."

"Is he the cove from Porthwellian Tredennick?" Tommy asked.

Peter said it was, although he wasn't sure. Denzil Porthwellian was a pisky halfling who *lived human*. He dealt with fay clients who sometimes needed advice with money. Peter understood money, but he understood the fay barter-favour system a lot better. He slid his hand in his pocket. Grandad Alexis handled the money for the family, and when Peter wanted to go *over there*, he got some from Alexis to pay for the pictures or tickets for dances. He knew Alexis, in turn, got the money from Denzil, and Denzil got it by investing money that people like Peter earned if they tried *living human* for a while. It seemed a mad system to him, but he knew if you went *over here*, you had to conform to the *over here* customs. Otherwise, you could get into all sorts of trouble.

"You might want to talk to him," Tommy said, and Peter agreed he would, sometime.

"Not that he's not honest. That's the firm Jude has her stuff with. Me, too, and the kiddies' trust. Straight as a die."

"What do you mean by trust?" Pia asked, sounding interested.

Tommy said, "I expect Jude will explain that, Missus Peckerdale. Look, why don't you come into town with us instead of walking? We're going to have a meal at the guesthouse café before we go to the gallery, and it'd be good to have some company. Besides, Jude has something she would like to do with Peter if Missus Peckerdale doesn't mind."

Peter opened his mouth to say Pia was *Mistress* Peckerdale but closed it again. He'd liked Judit, and her man seemed all right. He'd looked Pia over, but not that way. Peter thought any man alive would want to look at his miss. He wondered what old Thaddeus Appledore would have thought of her and concluded he'd have looked her over, too. He had an eye for beauty, which made it odd that he'd chosen to paint Peter and Judit, who wasn't a thousandth as beautiful as his Pia. He wished again that Thadd could have painted Pia.

I'd fucking love to have a picture of her.

He remembered there was a picture of him with Barbie somewhere. It wasn't a painting, though. It was a photograph someone from the art school took.

"What do you think, my miss? Want to go with these folks?" he asked.

"Let's! It'll be fun."

"We'll come. Thank you," Peter said.

They got in the back of the car, and Peter realised why it looked familiar. "This is old Thadd's car."

"It was ... technically, it belongs to you, but you never claimed it, so we thought it might as well get some use," Judit said.

"We were going to look for a car today," Pia put in.

"You'd better take this one."

"No, we want something small and green, and easy to hide," Peter said.

"And old," Pia said.

"You keep this. It's too fucking visible," Peter said.

Tommy laughed. "You can't just give a car away, Peter!"

"Of course, I can. Just did. You've kept it registered and all." He was proud of himself for remembering that detail.

"We'll give you the little runabout my mum gave us, then. It's just sitting in the shed at her place since she got her new one. Might need new tyres."

"What about that trust?" Pia asked.

Peter listened as Judit explained about money put away to earn more money for their sons when they were older. That sounded quite like the way Den Porthwellian handled their money *over here*, but he liked the idea of building something for his little miss and any other children they might have. Pia had said, during one of their oh fuck friendlies, that they ought to have an oxytocin friendly sometime soon. He gathered she thought they should make their next baby on purpose rather than by accident. He was happy with one little miss. He and Peter G were only children, and it seemed natural to him, but Pia had a sister. She wanted a bigger family, and therefore, so did he.

"We've invested in a bit of property, too, since I got a promotion," Tommy said.

Peter was interested in that, too. He knew land *over here* wasn't acquired by tree rule or favour as it was at home, but before he could ask for details, they'd arrived in Patterdale.

They shared a meal at a café in an old colonial guesthouse set in a pretty garden.

Peter was negotiating something that was supposed to be a pie but which didn't taste like one when Pia nudged him. He turned to her immediately. "What's wrong, my miss?"

"Nothing, dear. This is a nice place, don't you think? Happy. Warm."

He gathered she wasn't talking about the temperature. He focused on the atmosphere of the place and found he agreed. The jangle and fuss of *over here* was barely perceptible. "Wonder if it's warded?"

"No-o. Just nice. Who owns it?" Pia asked Judit.

"I don't know. Why?"

"Wondered if they were fucking fairies," Peter explained. Judit choked.

Pia sighed. "Peter, did you ever do disclosure with Judit?"

He shook his head. He hadn't done disclosure with anyone, except Barbie, who had guessed anyway, and who had told her brother, who had then got too interested in his blood.

"Fuck," he said.

Judit gave him the indulgent smile he remembered from

their time with Thaddeus. "Want to explain yourself, Peter? I gather you're not talking about being *that way.*"

"Not really. No."

Pia gave him a *look* and said, "I'll do disclosure." She got hold of Peter's arm and conjured his sleeve up.

Peter reflected that usually, he loved it when she bared his body because that meant a friendly was going to happen, but this time he resented it. He conjured the sleeve down.

"Peter." She sounded as if she was preparing to be difficult.

Sulkily, he rolled it up, and reluctantly, he looked up to see Judit and her man staring at him.

"Do it," Pia said.

He put two fingers on his inner elbow and *rubbed up the green.* Then he took his hand away. "There."

"What does that prove?" Tommy asked, staring at the green patch of skin the friction had produced.

"I'm a fucking pixie. Pureblood. So's my miss, but she doesn't rub up as well. The misses don't."

Judit put both hands over her mouth and choked again.

"Are you all right?" Pia asked.

Judit nodded, her dark eyes wide. Then she said in a whisper to Tommy, "I *said* he was green down there, remember."

Peter gave her an unfriendly look. "If you want to talk about my bits in private, you'd better do it more quietly. We have better hearing than you think."

Pia, eyes dancing, said, "I suppose you saw his willy when he was being the swan man for the painting. It's usually only green when he's er — "

"Embarrassed," Peter said quickly.

Pia giggled. "That, too, but he doesn't often get embarrassed."

"Really pixies?" Tommy said. His eyebrows said more.

"Really pixies," Pia said.

"Like . . . *tündérek*?" Judit asked.

"Don't know them. Where do they live?"

"Hungarian fairies." Tommy indicated his wife. "Jude was born in Hungary."

Judit said cautiously, "I don't think the people who own this place are fairies, but then, I didn't know you were."

"Might ask them," Peter said, looking about for the woman who'd brought the pie.

"Not today," Pia said, touching his arm in what he took to be an apology. "We need to finish eating."

Peter went back to the pie, but now Pia had brought it to his attention, he felt the building warm and welcoming around him.

They paid for their meals and walked along to the gallery to see the retrospective. As Tommy had mentioned, Judit had a favour to ask, and she asked it in the foyer where Tommy was explaining to an officious woman why they didn't need to buy tickets.

"Peter, Tommy likes to play games sometimes, and he thought it would be fun if people recognised you and me from the painting," Judit said.

Peter hadn't thought that far. People at the art school had recognised him, of course, since a lot of them had drawn him.

"They'll recognise you as soon as they see you near the painting. You're distinctive-looking."

"My Peter is beautiful," Pia said.

Judit gave her a startled look and examined Peter with more attention. "He is, isn't he? When I knew him before he was a bit . . . wistful. Now he looks happy, even when he's glaring at me."

"That's because I am happy. I have my miss and my little miss," Peter growled.

"What did you want to ask?" Pia asked as Tommy came over to say they were free to enter.

"We had no idea you'd be here, but when we were talking

about it ages ago, we thought it might be fun if I gave you a kiss in front of the painting . . . just to stir people up a bit."

"And then *I'll* give her a kiss, and you can kiss Pia, Peter," Tommy said cheerfully. Obviously, he knew exactly what was being discussed. "Is that all right with you, Pia?"

"Of course," Pia said. She gave Peter a mischievous look. "And I'll kiss *you,* Tommy, and you can kiss Peter, and I'll kiss Judit."

Peter cringed inside, but his miss had spoken, and so he acquiesced. "*No harm.*"

Tommy raised his eyebrows. "Judit, my love, you've created a monster."

"No, *we* have. But let's do it. Half the people in here think artists' models are immoral anyway. Let's give them something to talk about."

They entered the gallery, which had two floors. Peter stared at the paintings around the walls. He'd seen some of Thadd's work, but those had been rough sketches. The painted canvases on display were much bigger.

It wasn't just paintings, though. There were also smaller framed sketches and half-coloured drawings.

One group caught his eye, and he recognised himself, head and shoulder, hand, torso, legs. There were some sketches of Judit, too, waif-like, wispy and light. They moved on to older canvases showing people Peter didn't know. There were old men and women, a savage rendition of a middle-aged man, and a couple that looked as if Thadd had painted himself looking into a mirror.

Peter looked away from those. The old man he'd known had burned with the ambition to create one final piece of work. The man in the self-portraits seemed to burn with unhappiness.

Then he saw one of Judit kneeling, one arm upstretched, the other curved around herself. She was obviously expecting a child.

"First ever portrait of our little Tolly," Judit said cheerfully.

Her husband stared. "God, you were beautiful then. That must have been . . . what . . . a few weeks before he was born?"

"A few *days*," Judit said. "Mister Appledore said I wasn't to *have that kid* until he finished painting."

"I'm buying that. And that." He pointed to another painting, showing Judit standing under a stream of water, poured down by a shadowy figure with an urn.

"He heated it for me," Judit said. She indicated the second figure. "That's me, too, when I was nineteen. It was Simone doing the pouring really, but she's busty, so Mister A made us change poses and combined the sketches. There should be another matching one of Simone."

Maybe there was, but Peter didn't see it.

He thought Judit looked like a water maid, although she was wearing a petticoat and they usually didn't.

"I'll have that one, too," Tommy said.

"He's like a kiddy in a sweet shop. He's got me already, so why's he want these?" Judit said to Pia.

"Because they're fucking gorgeous," Peter said. He felt an odd twinge of sadness and guilt. He'd been thinking Judit very ordinary next to his perfect miss, and now he saw she had beauty. "Bloody old Thad, eh?" He felt the prickle of tears and stopped speaking, appalled. He cried sometimes, often with happiness, but this was the human world, where men just didn't.

"Let's go and look at the *Swansong*," Judit said, hauling Tommy away from the pictures of her younger self.

Peter followed with Pia.

The swansong triptych was even bigger than Peter remembered. He stared at it, speechless, as forgotten details of his time spent posing came to mind.

In the first panel, Judit's Leda lay half-raised from a cushion that was obviously meant to be a mossy bank. She seemed to be waking, stretching, and half-smiling in profile. Peter's swan man stood out of her line of vision, staring. The face was fixed in a look of yearning. It was unmistakably his, but older, more the age he was now.

In the second panel, Leda cowered, curled into a defensive bundle, while Peter's swan man loomed, curved over her with shadowy wings.

In the third, both faces were visible, with Leda ecstatic and the swan man haunted with despair.

Tommy said, "My God."

Judit put her hand on his arm. "Told you it was big."

Peter just stared, clutching Pia's hand.

They stood awhile until someone cleared her throat behind them. "Excuse me . . . would you mind moving on so we can see?"

Peter turned around to face a startled woman. Her mouth opened in astonishment.

"It's you—you're the swan!" she said loudly.

Other people turned to look.

Peter remembered what he had to do. He let go of Pia and turned to Judit. "Judit! I've got to kiss you!"

She stared at him for a moment and then swung into action. "Peter!" she yelled in a loud dramatic tone. "*Darlink!*" She flung her arms around him, kicking one leg out behind her.

Peter found himself with an armful that reminded him disturbingly of the little tree maids he'd sometimes hugged in his teens. Then his body remembered. He'd stood patiently supporting Judit for hours. He closed his arms in a hug and kissed her brow. "*No harm*, Judit."

"You used to say that back then, and of course not." She laughed softly. "Can you be a bit more convincing? Tommy really gets turned on by this."

He picked her up and tipped her back, falling into the looming pose of the swan. Judit, choking with laughter, raised her arm and let her head fall back to expose her throat. They held the pose until Judit said, "Ouch," and then Peter lifted her upright and set her on her feet. He pushed her to her husband and gladly hugged Pia. "My miss, my *fucking gorgeous* miss."

Tommy tapped him on the shoulder. "My turn." The man's eyes sparked with mischief. He took Pia and kissed her cheek.

Pia turned to Judit, and they hugged.

Tommy put his hands on Peter's shoulders. "You're being a good sport about this, but I won't ask you to snog me. Just a hug, eh?"

Peter hugged him. "*No harm. No harm.*"

"We ought to buy this," Tommy said when they broke the hug, and the clamour and fuss had died away, helped considerably by the glamour Peter cast to shut out the racket.

Judit said, "Can't do that, love. It's *reserved.* All the practice ones of Peter and me are, too." She shrugged. "Never mind. Maybe we can get a photo of it each. They might do some prints, too."

Tommy flexed his fingers. "Let's hope so. I want everyone to see this."

Peter thought he was crazy. Good man, full of love for his wife, but crazy. He whispered to Pia, "You wouldn't want to see *that* every day."

"No. But I'm so glad we saw it today."

It took them a while to get out of the gallery because Peter and Judit were seized on by odd people pushing cards into their hands and wanting to *give them a ring* about further work.

One woman said quietly to Peter that he should speak with her before he signed *anything,* dearie. "Don't put yourself about too much. You need to be choosy."

She had a sweet face under too much make-up, so Peter took her card.

She drew in a deep breath and said in an even quieter voice, "You're a fairy, aren't you, dear. I thought so when I first saw those sketches Thadd sent me back in nineteen fifty."

"Pixie," Peter said. Then he added, "You knew old Thadd?"

"Never met him, but we corresponded for years." She grimaced. "I live just outside Perth, and we were always going to meet one day and swap scurrilous stories. Then the drink got him, and by the time I heard that he'd passed over, it was all over red rover. He left me a painting in his will, the old reprobate. Very naughty. But dear, I'm serious about signing things. I know Thadd thought a lot of you, and he was tickled pink to have you under an exclusive. Thing is, he didn't exploit you . . ." She sounded vaguely questioning.

"We were friends."

"That's good, but there are sharks out there in the waters, so you take care."

Peter held out his hand. "Thank you, mistress."

"I haven't heard that in a while and I'm not sure I merit it. My name's Magda Quest. My mother's an alpenfee quarterling." She squeezed his hand and said, "Stay happy, Peter."

"You, too," he said.

She gave him a surprisingly merry grin. "I make it my business to be happy. I have a few kissing cousins *over there,* and I get over to see them once in a while. Mum's still with us, and she can open the gates, so we go together. Once she passes, I'll have to find someone else with enough of the blood to do the honours."

"There's a gate not far from here," Peter said.

"Well! I wish I'd known that years ago. Could have come through to visit Thadd."

Chapter Nineteen: Smooch

The Guesthouse, Patterdale. 1955
Peter Peckerdale

"What now?" Judit asked Peter and Pia as they left the gallery.

"We can give you the runabout, but I'm not sure about the tyres. Could get some new ones on if you're still here in the morning," Tommy said.

"You're welcome to a bed at our place if you don't mind the couch," Judit offered.

Pia tugged Peter's arm. "That café place has rooms. Could we stay there?"

He looked down into her hopeful face in the odd light coming from a high pole. "What about our miss?"

"She'll be asleep soon anyway. Mum and Dad love having her. They get a bit lonely now Alba's wed to Farran."

Peter recalled Alba's wedding, at which Rory Inkersoll had officiated. He recalled eyeing Farran Willow, Alba's man, and wondering what Gard had said to *him*. He hoped it had been scary. He'd come to understand it was a pixie father's duty to try to scare any man who wanted his little miss.

Just wait until some green-willied fucker wants our Melody.

"Peter?"

"You want to sleep there, my miss?"

"Yes, please."

The guesthouse was close to the gallery, so Tommy and Judit walked them over. Judit said it might be fully booked, on

165

account of the retrospective.

"You can come to us if it is," she said.

Peter hoped it wouldn't come to that. He'd quite enjoyed his time with the Creeds, but he wanted to be alone with his miss.

They went back into the guesthouse and the warmth wrapped around them.

"Back again?" The woman who'd served their meal smiled pleasantly. Her name tag read *Eunice*.

"Do you have a room we can have tonight?"

Regret came over her face. "I'm sorry . . . there's just one tiny room left, and that's right at the top of the house. It couldn't possibly sleep four."

"We're off home anyway," Judit said cheerfully.

Pia squeezed Peter's arm.

"We'll have that," Peter said.

Tommy clapped Peter on the shoulder. "We'll see you folks in the morning, about ten. I'll get the tyres checked on the runabout, and then Jude can drive it here, and I'll take her home in the big one."

Peter remembered to shake hands with Tommy, and, since she seemed to expect it, he kissed Judit on the cheek.

"See you tomorrow, Peter, and thanks for being a good sport and giving Tommy a thrill back there."

Peter signed the register and was pleased to learn that a light supper and breakfast were included in the modest price.

"Up two flights of stairs. It's right at the top," the woman said. She looked behind them. "No bags?"

"No, we meant to go home tonight, but we've decided to stay instead to get a car in the morning," Pia said.

"Wait a bit, then, and I'll get your supper things. Save me walking upstairs later." The woman went off into what was presumably the kitchen and came back after a while with a jug of milk, some biscuits, cheese and sandwiches. "There's a kettle and some plates and things there. The key's in the lock. Take it out, and then you can put it back there in the morning," she said, handing the tray to Peter.

Peter let Pia precede him up the narrow stairs. This was her idea, and he wanted her to enjoy the first sight of the room.

The woman was right. It was small, but it had a tiny bathroom and a table with two chairs. The kettle was electric, but Peter remembered how to use it from his days at *Lady Lydia Appledore House*.

They had supper and washed, and then Pia went over to the bed, conjured off her tunic and got in.

Peter followed suit. He was about to snuggle her into their usual sleeping position when he remembered what she'd said to him once. He could suggest. He didn't have to wait for her.

"My miss, would you like a friendly?"

"I'd *love* one." Pia kissed him and then put one hand on his willy. "Peter, do you remember we talked about having another baby?"

"Yes, of course. You said you'd tell me when it was time."

She fondled his balls. "It's time."

No oh-fuck friendly, then. He was a little disappointed.

Then Pia said, "I thought we might have an oh-fuck friendly first. Then, when you're ready, we can make a baby. We'll have to both remember to *do oxytocin*." That was her term for *not* holding hard or closing off whatever she usually did.

"Why two?" he asked and added quickly, "Not that I'm complaining. I fucking love it, you know."

"I thought an *oh-fuck* friendly would loosen me up. That way you'll be able to slide in, and we can think of lovely things for our baby instead of wondering how to fit you in." She ran her fingers along his willy. "Better stop talking before you go and spill. We'll do you first. Then you'll have some time to get ready again while we do me."

Peter rolled onto his back.

Pia switched around in the bed and went on fondling him. He bit his tongue.

Don't let go.

Ahhhh . . .

She put her mouth over him, rubbing his balls so that he relaxed into the sensations. As usual, he wanted it to go on forever. As usual, he fought the build-up, and as usual, he lost the fight.

He gasped. "Oh-oh-fuck, that's — oh — " He tried breathing shallowly.

Pia lifted away and gave his willy a two-fingered smack. "Stop that, my Peter. Just enjoy it. You *know* you can have it again, and again, whenever you want. There's no need to put it off or ration it out."

He couldn't speak, but she'd apparently finished what she had to say, because she went back to sucking and rubbing.

He stopped fighting. "Oh-fuck-oh-fuck-oh-*fuck* . . ."

He spurted, and now he wasn't trying to hold back, he enjoyed the wonderful feeling of release. His miss was right, as ever. This exquisite pleasure was his whenever he needed it. She went on fondling him, kissing him dreamily until he remembered he had more to do.

"Your turn, my miss. Would you like a pixie smooch?"

Pia said, "I'd *love* a pixie smooch. Maybe use two fingers, to stretch things a bit?"

Peter conjured a pillow under her hips and configured his mouth for kissing. Then he had an idea. "Pia, what if we do something a bit different? When you're nearly ready, I can switch over, and we'll do an oxytocin."

"Will you be able to do that so soon?"

"You could always put a willy-tingler on me."

"I could if you like, but — "

She sounded doubtful, so he said, "I'll be ready, anyway."

"All right, we'll try that, but please start soon, or I'll be dripping all over the sheets."

He laughed and gently kissed her, using one finger and then adding another. When he felt the first flutter of a squeeze on his hand, he quickly got to his knees, moved up and slid into her.

She gasped, but not with pain. "Smooch me!"

He attended to her lips, feeling himself expanding in her tight nether grip.

I wonder if fucking old Thadd would have painted this?

He remembered the old man's words when he'd been finishing the triptych.

My life's not been wasted, in any event. I might be a scrawny old queer without blood of my own, but I've given beauty to the world.

No blood of his own. How sad. This one's for you, my old friend.

Then he stopped thinking, gathered the greatest joy in his life closer still, unleashed everything he had and *gave*.

Chapter Twenty: Kristos

The Cottage, Pixie Forest. 1956
Pia Peckerdale

Pia was determined that Peter would receive their son into his hands and hold her through the pain at the same time.

Peter, apparently knowing better than to argue, said he would, but only if Melody was elsewhere. "Your mum or mine can look after her."

"No," Pia said.

"But they often do."

"I don't want them to know we're having your son until he's here." She saw Peter about to object and said, "This is our business. It's going to hurt a lot, and I don't want them thinking about it or talking about it, or sending notes to see how we're progressing. I also don't want them sending me a water maid to help. I want you."

"All right. Peter G and Joe can look after her. They won't think or talk about it because they don't know how it works."

"Good. Yes. As soon as the pains start, you sent a message to Peter G, and he can get Joe if he's here. They can take Melody for a picnic."

Joe was a pixie quarterling, but he couldn't conjure yet, and Peter said he probably never would.

Joe had other talents. He was warm and kind and musical. Pia had no problem with Peter G and Joe minding Melody, who would be delighted to have two big boys to order around.

Her pains started after breakfast, which was a good thing, because it gave Peter time to get Peter G and Joe without occasioning questions as to why he required them to mind his little miss in the middle of the night.

The boys brought Melody in to say goodbye. Pia was already sweating with pain. Peter G said cheerfully, "Come on, Melly, let's go and see the butterflies in the alpen meadow. Joe will come out later, maybe."

Joe came over to the bed. He was a lanky lad with brown hair and tea-coloured eyes and olive pixie skin. He said softly, "I have a bit of healing talent, and Master Peckerdale said I might be able to help."

"I don't need healing." Pia clenched her fists. "I'm all right."

Peter, looking as pale as his skin could manage, said, "Of course you're all right, but Joe might be able to help. Just let him . . ." He nodded to Joe.

Pia glared at him. "I want you. I told you."

"And you've got me."

Joe said gently, "Mum gets a backache sometimes. She's a halfling, and she says I have magic hands. If you'd like to cuddle up to your man, I can give you a little bit of warmth. Is that all right?"

A savage pain racked Pia, and she gritted her teeth. "Yes."

Peter conjured his clothing off, just as if the boy wasn't there, and got in with Pia. He put his arms around her and tucked her against him.

Pia heard Joe rubbing his hands together, and then he placed his palms on her back where the pain was worst.

"I can't stop it, Mistress Peckerdale, because you need it to happen, but I can help you relax a bit."

Pia caught her breath as warmth spread from his hands. He smelled comfortingly of hay.

He said, still quietly, "Are you having another little girl like

Melody, or do you think you might have a boy?"

"A son," Pia said. The pain receded, and she kissed Peter's throat, relaxing against him.

"That's nice. Mum only ever had me, but she said it was nice having a son."

The pain came again, but this time the warmth kept it at bay before it peaked.

Pia felt Peter's anxiety receding, too. Warmth flowed from him, and she kissed him again, with more attention.

Joe said, "There, Peter, you've got it, too, so can you keep this going?"

"Yes, I'll fucking well do it if it kills me."

"We'll just do one more then, and then the little fellow will feel better, too. What are you going to call him?"

Pia felt her muscles tightening, but the warm hands smoothed it aside.

"What's your other name?" Peter asked.

"What? Bakewell? Dad's human. It's a funny name, but I like it. It's a kind of tart and a place in England."

"No. Middle name."

"Oh. Kristos. It's Greek. Dad's grandmother is Greek, and she wanted me to have her name, too. It's a Greek form of Christopher. He was a saint. That's another reason my skin is dark."

Peter said, "That's a fucking good name. Like it, my miss?"

Pia was so grateful that she thought she'd agree to anything.

"I like that. It's lovely," she said. Then she said in a rush, "I have to push!"

"I'll leave you to manage this bit, Peter," Joe said. He moved back and then bent over and kissed Pia's brow. He stepped away.

The door closed quietly.

"The way we did it before?" Peter asked.

She nodded. He rolled onto his back, conjured pillows and got her into position.

"All right, darling, I'm ready."

Pia said, dazed, "It's not taking long this time."

"Long enough, my love."

A surge hit her, and she pushed, hard and steadily.

"Got him."

Again . . .

She panted with effort and *pushed*.

Peter said, "Fucking wonderful, here he comes . . . Greet you, Kristos!"

"Kiss him," she managed to say as she flopped, panting and laughing.

Peter kissed him. "Time."

"Time what? Is it getting dark? Where did the day go? Oh, give him to me."

"Not time, thyme." He pronounced a phantom T as he clicked up a lantern.

Pia rolled down into the bed, bringing the baby with her. Peter was right. Their new son smelled of thyme, and it seemed his name was Kristos.

Kristos Peter Peckerdale. It was a strong name, with a little gentleness about it. She liked it. She *loved* it. And her darling Peter was crying tears of joy.

The story continues in *Peter G and Gentian*

You may also enjoy the following from eXtasy Books Inc:

Queen of the May
Lark Westerly

Excerpt

When she was sixteen, Lucy Tan tumbled into love with August Herron.

In the classroom, she spent long dreamy periods learning every line of his face, watching his deft movements, and bathing in his air of sparkling enthusiasm.

She learned to split her attention, so half of her was intelligent, studious Lucy, applying herself to projects and assignments, answering questions and volunteering well-formed opinions. The other half spent those same classes inventing scenarios where she helped him with something important, and he kissed her and then they—

And then he'd be mortified because teachers aren't allowed to kiss students.

Okay, so she helped him, and he gave her a special smile.

Class was ending. She was vaguely aware of Nelis Winter packing away her notes across the aisle.

Someone rustled busily away behind her. She smelled a waft of marmalade.

One of the fay . . . and probably a full blood.

Special smile . . .

God, Lucy, what are you? Nine? Special smile indeed.

A long, slow meeting of eyes?

God, Lucy, you're so —

She couldn't think what she was.

Desperate.

"Lucy?"

Oh God!

He'd spoken to her, and she hadn't heard. She cast her mind back, hoping some residual echo might tell her what he'd said.

"Lucy?" August Herron gave her a quizzical smile. Her name sounded lovely in his soft voice, with the little upwards tilt.

"I'm sorry, Mister Herron. I was thinking about something else."

I should say, Master Herron. That way you'd know I know what you are.

Lu-cy, don't be an idiot. He doesn't care what you know. He barely even bothers to glamour his ears. A quarter of this class has at least one fairy in the family pot . . .

Mercifully, he just smiled and repeated the question, coming down from his desk On High to stand beside her as the classroom emptied around them.

Ohhhh, you smell so good! Broad bean flowers . . .

"Are you up for the lead in Queen of the May?"

She got up in an undignified scramble, feeling sweat forming between her shoulders.

Don't smile too broadly. It makes your eyes disappear.

He wasn't a tall man, but even standing, the top of her head was about level with his chin.

"Why?" She knew she sounded wary, but she had to get this right. He didn't teach drama, so what reason could he have for wanting to know?

"If you are, then the best of luck. I think you'd nail it."

She blinked.

"But if you're not, or if you're going for a smaller part, I'd like you to help me with set design."

"I'd love to."

"Great. Let me know as soon as you decide."

Lucy had already auditioned. She'd been singing and dancing since she was four, and she knew she was good. The musical was the story of a modern girl who found herself in Merrie England, where, over her protestations of sexism and exploitation, she was crowned Queen of the May and used her influence to improve the lot of the village maidens. It was fluffy and dated, but it had lots of parts, and Bess, the heroine, had some amusing solos. The finale, called Beat of My Own Drum, would really weed out the competition. Bess had to carry a strong melody line above a chorus of thirty singing a different tune.

Despite her powerful singing voice, Lucy knew she had little hope of playing Bess, who spent one whole soliloquy pointing out that she stood taller than all the guys.

She had run through the scene at the auditions to predictable jeers from boys, who said yes, if they were on their knees . . .

It hurt. She wanted to be Bess.

Grow up, Lucy. No matter how hard you work, you won't grow a head taller and be big, blonde and beautiful. You'll be cast as a village urchin . . . or maybe the comedy pedlar girl. Being passed over because you're not a good-enough singer or actor is one thing, but being passed over because of your genes is worse. You can improve your skills, but if you're short and mostly Chinese, you're short . . . and mostly Chinese.

Now, of course, she was glad she wouldn't get the part. Helping Master August Herron with set design? Yes, please. She was dancing on air, and she wondered why she hadn't said yes right away.

Drama was the last class of the day. After the siren wailed,

Jenny Shackleton said, "Lucy, a word."

"Yes, Ms Shackleton." She stayed behind as Miffy and Melanie Smith, the ill-assorted cousins, clumped noisily past her.

"You're in for it now, Tan," Melanie muttered, more in hope than from conviction.

Lucy frowned. The teachers of Diversity High seldom told one off in public. They were much more likely to ask for help with a trifling task . . . and then unleash on the luckless student.

But I can't be in trouble. I haven't done anything. Or am I in trouble for fibbing about the audition? I didn't tell Mister Herron I hadn't auditioned. I said . . .

Her thoughts tangled.

Ms Shackleton shooed out the cousins, who showed signs of hopeful lingering, and closed the door firmly behind them.

"Am I in trouble, Ms Shackleton?"

Jenny Shackleton smiled. "Not at all. I just wanted to give you the heads up before I finalise the cast list . . . I'd like you to play Bess."

For a moment, the words made no sense, and then Lucy felt a surge of astonished delight. Then she remembered lovely Mister Herron and the sets.

She couldn't do both. All sections of work on the Year Eleven musical occupied the same time-blocks.

She gave herself a few seconds to envisage each scenario and came to the only decision she could countenance.

"No, thanks, Ms Shackleton."

Jenny Shackleton's face, which had been benevolent and smiling, blanked in amazement.

A penny dropped with a small, almost audible, chink.

Offering the part to me is some kind of policy statement.

"I'm nothing like the way Bess describes herself in the songs."

Ms Shackleton relaxed. "Oh, I think we can get around that. Maybe we can put you up on a table when you sing stand taller, or you might sing smaller rather than taller? And intelligent and dutiful instead of big, blonde and beautiful. Yes, why not? We don't want to emphasise the popular concept of physical beauty."

No, we don't, do we. Even though the script clearly does it in an ironic way.

You don't truly believe I'm best for the part. You're just making a point by casting a small, dark girl of Asian appearance as a Queen of the May and maybe sticking up two fingers at those idiotic boys with their down on their knees comments.

Well, I'm no one's point and no one's poster person.

She said, stiffly, "I don't think so, thank you. There's still the England's Rose song, and I don't think someone who looks the way I do would have been crowned as May Queen in Merrie England, do you? This reeks of positive discrimination to me."

Ms Shackleton flushed a deep, plum red and said, "That's a very cynical view, Lucy. Here at Diversity, we believe in absolute equality."

"But we're not equal, Ms Shackleton. Some of us are better than others."

She meant to expand on her theory about the need for the quintet of talent, dedication, genetic disposition, environment and desire, but Ms Shackleton was going all tight-jawed.

"If that's your attitude, I'll withdraw the offer."

"I could fit in one of the smaller parts," Lucy ventured.

"They're already cast."

"But you'll have to upgrade someone . . . or . . ."

"Thank you, Lucy. I don't need any more of your condescension."

Lucy hurried out, cheeks stinging, pretending not to see Melanie and Miffy still lingering.

The sting faded as she strode around the visual arts classroom.

August Herron wasn't there.

Of course. He has appointments from three-thirty every day.

As well as teaching visual arts and PD, Mister Herron was the school counsellor. It was only a few minutes after three, and the screen was still open in the little privacy alcove, so she went to tap on his office door.

"Come in."

She opened the door.

"You're a bit early, but I'll be with you in a minute. Help yourself to coffee—" He looked up with a professional smile from the papers he was sorting. "Oh, Lucy. I thought you were my three-thirty." His smile turned genuine. "What can I do for you?"

She glanced behind him at the wall full of cups and mugs. Flowers and cartoons, birds, slogans, dogs . . . she was tempted to take him up on the offer of coffee, but she didn't want to get mixed up with his three-thirty.

"I came to tell you I've decided. I'm not in the musical . . . well, not in a role."

I won't even make the chorus, if Ms Shackleton can help it.

"I hope you're not too disappointed."

"Oh, no! I'd much rather help you." She sought for something more grown-up. "I mean . . . realistically, I'm never going to make a career out of acting, but a set design project is good experience for a lot of jobs."

"You see yourself in this area of work, then?"

She hadn't, but now she did. Again, she sought for the best spin.

"I haven't decided yet, but I'd like broad experience in creation and innovation . . . maybe even teaching or organising projects."

He nodded. "That's how I came to be in my position. My two positions. I'd love to discuss your options further with you. We'll arrange a get-together appointment."

"But I don't—"

He laughed, making her skin tingle. "Not a counselling

appointment, Lucy. You seem to have your life on-track already. I just meant some general brainstorming on career choices."

Someone tapped on the door.

"Five minutes!" he called out. Then he said to Lucy, "For now, we'll concentrate on the set design. Welcome aboard. Can you be here well before school on Thursday?"

"Yes."

"By seven-thirty? We'll make it a breakfast meeting. It'll be a one-off. The rest of the design will double-deck with the drama classes."

"No problems."

Have to catch an early train.

They smiled at one another, and he took her hand briefly.

Mister Herron was anything but touchy-feelie, but unlike most of the teachers, he didn't shy away from the occasional contact. His hand was warm, and Lucy had to force herself not to cling.

"Tomorrow, Lucy," he said, and it sounded like a promise.

Lucy let herself out of the office. She didn't look at the little alcove where August's counselling students waited, but she knew the screen was drawn. She called softly, "Mister Herron is free now. I'm sure he'll know how to help you."

A choked sob acknowledged her.

Poor you, whoever you are.

She hurried off, with Mister Herron's voice ringing in her memory.

You seem to have your life on-track already. Tomorrow, Lucy.

Lucy caught the six-thirty train on Thursday morning and arrived at the office door by twenty-past. Nelis Winter, Sierra Sinclair, and Toshi Kahn were there. A couple of minutes later, an odd, eager new boy, whose name was Xavier Partridge but whom everyone called Bird Boy, arrived with Mister Herron. They were carrying baskets of something that smelled good.

Lucy realised, with a sinking feeling, that they were all here for the breakfast meeting.

So much for the two of us working one-on-one. Maybe I should have said Yes to Ms Shackleton . . . I could have been Queen of the May.

She put the thought away.

Working alongside August Herron on a challenging project was wonderful anyway, even with all those others. It gave her a secret buzz that lasted right up to the end of the school year, but she never forgot she might have been Queen of the May.

ABOUT THE AUTHOR

Lark Westerly loves creating worlds and series where characters step in and out of one another's stories. When she's not orchestrating the lives of these characters, Lark enjoys walking with her dogs, cultivating her websites, and cooking her own recipe creations. Under another name, Lark writes children's books and runs a small manuscript service.

For more about *A Fairy in the Bed* series, visit Lark's website at www.larksinger.weebly.com

www.ingramcontent.com/pod-product-compliance
Lightning Source LLC
Chambersburg PA
CBHW060815120626

46557CB00001B/230